Diary of a Tee

Caitlin Book N°. 3

WHO I AM

a novel

MELODY CARLSON

Multnomah®Publishers *Sisters, Oregon*

WHO I AM
published by Multnomah Publishers, Inc.
© 2002 by Melody Carlson

International Standard Book Number: 1-57673-890-6

Cover design by David Carlson Design
Cover image by Tony Stone Images
Cover image of flower by Photodisc

Scripture quotations are from:
The Holy Bible, New International Version © 1973, 1984 by International Bible
Society, used by permission of Zondervan Publishing House

Multnomah is a trademark of Multnomah Publishers, Inc.,
and is registered in the U.S. Patent and Trademark Office.
The colophon is a trademark of Multnomah Publishers, Inc.

Printed in the United States of America

For information:
MULTNOMAH PUBLISHERS, INC.
POST OFFICE BOX 1720
SISTERS, OREGON 97759

Library of Congress Cataloging-in-Publication Data
Carlson, Melody.
  Who I am, by Caitlin O'Conner / Melody Carlson.
  ISBN 1-57673-890-6 (pbk.)
  I. Title.
PZ7.C216637 Wj 2002   2001007013

04 05 06 07—10 9 8 7 6 5 4

PRAISE FOR MELODY CARLSON'S

Diary of a Teenage Girl, Caitlin Book 2:

It's My Life

"Melody Carlson creates a cast of characters who are real and engaging. It made me want to read the first book in the series and hope that there will be more!"

NANCY RUE, BESTSELLING AUTHOR OF *HERE'S LILY!* AND *LILY THE REBEL*

"Melody has done it again! Teens won't be able to resist Caitlin's latest diary. Teens will identify and laugh with Caitlin and gain spiritual insight from this fresh glimpse into the heart of a very real teenage girl."

HEATHER KOPP, AUTHOR OF *LOVE STORIES GOD TOLD*
AND *I STOLE GOD FROM GOODY TWO-SHOES*

"This book inspired me to persevere through all my hardships and struggles, but it also brought me to the reality that even through my flaws, God can make Himself known in a powerful, life-changing way."

MEGHAN MCAULAY, FOURTEEN-YEAR-OLD REVIEWER

"I definitely recommend the book *It's My Life* to teens. Even if you haven't read the first book, it's very easy to pick up what's going on. I was surprised at how easily I could relate my own life to Caitlin's. I really got involved with the book. I could hardly put it down!"

HEATHER SCHWARZBURG, SIXTEEN-YEAR-OLD REVIEWER

"What an awesome way to convey what teenagers are faced with in today's world. *It's My Life* captures the expressions and feelings every teenager may face and the struggle they battle within themselves trying to find a solution. A must-read for not only the teens but adults too."

KORINA MOYER, YOUTH STAFF VOLUNTEER

Diary of a Teenage Girl, Caitlin Book 1:

Becoming Me

"As I read through *Diary of a Teenage Girl,* I had to keep reminding myself that I wasn't reading my own diary! It captures the thoughts and issues of a teenager's struggles to follow God's pathway."

RACHAEL LAMPA, TEEN RECORDING ARTIST

"From the first page, *Diary* captured me. I couldn't stop reading! This is a brilliant, well-crafted imaginary journey to the heart of a sixteen-year-old. I can't wait for the sequel!"

"As I read *Diary*…I felt as if I had been given a gift—a 'backstage pass' into the life and heart of Caitlin O'Conner. It is a wonderful and mysterious ride as we are allowed a rare chance to travel alongside a teenage girl as she lives in the real world. This is a unique and refreshing read—fun and entertaining, while at the same time moving and insightful. Read and learn."

"Creative and impactful! *Diary* drew me in as my concern for Caitlin and her friends grew stronger each page I turned. It gave me the inside story to issues I see in my own life—and among my friends and peers. I recommend this book to every teenage girl going through the struggles of peer pressure, dating, and other temptations we face in life."

"Melody Carlson writes with the clear, crisp voice of today's adolescent. *Diary of a Teenage Girl* is sure to please any teenager who is struggling with peer pressure, identity, and a desire to know and understand God's will. A moving, tender story that will be remembered…and loved."

"Melody Carlson captures the voice of teens today in a character we can all relate to. The unique peer perspective makes it very effective. Integrating the crucial message of the gospel, it forces us to weigh issues and causes us to look at a young person—in reality, ourselves—objectively. It challenges, convicts, and leaves us with hope for the future. I highly recommend this book."

"Carlson succeeds in weaving Christian beliefs into the plot with a light hand—and it's a darn good read!"

ONE

Tuesday (after the missions conference)

It's a brand-new year, and it seems appropriate that I should begin a new diary today. And yet, to be perfectly honest, I don't feel much like writing. I know that seems crazy since so much has happened in the last few days—like I should be blabbering on for pages and pages. But I guess I'm feeling a little bummed right now or maybe just confused. And even that doesn't make sense, because I've had such an unbelievably awesome time here at Urbana. I mean, I've heard and seen more about worldwide missions than I'd ever imagined possible. And it almost blows your mind to see how many organizations exist! Still, that doesn't exactly explain this weird mix of emotions I'm having. To start with, I feel pretty small and insignificant at the moment (and I realize how self-centered that sounds). But it's the truth, and I guess it's because I'm just one among thousands of young people who God might be calling to some sort of missions opportunity somewhere around the globe.

I know it doesn't make sense. (I should be glad that so many kids really want to serve God.) Maybe I'm just tired and ready to go home. Or maybe I'm feeling a little slighted that Josh Miller has been so obsessed with the conference that he acts as if I don't even exist. Now how's that for shallow? (On my part, I mean.) Not to mention painfully honest! Okay, I know, I've made this big commitment not to date, and I'm trying really hard to stick to it, but, sheesh, how does it make a girl feel when someone like Josh won't even give her the time of day? Wasn't it just a year ago that Josh (my number-one hottee) was first getting interested in me—little Miss Nobody? And look at us now. It's almost funny. And yet...

Thankfully, we're about to hit the road! But before I sign off on New Year's Day sounding so gloomy, I must admit I do feel somewhat hopeful too. And I did get the chance to talk with several missions groups who focus on helping the most impoverished children, kind of like the kids at the dump in Mexico. As it turns out (sad as it seems) children who live at garbage dumps aren't all that uncommon (especially in Latin America). And so, I gathered up all these brochures and e-mail addresses and stuff, and I'll be communicating with the missions groups for more information and advice (not to mention praying that God will lead me!). And that all seems pretty worthwhile.

And if it wasn't for that, I'd probably be feeling pretty discouraged right now. There were times when I actually wondered why I'd come to this conference. Because almost every missions person I spoke with kept saying, "You need to go to college before you seriously consider going to work in Mexico or anywhere else." One old guy practically read me the riot act; he said it was "inexperienced people like me that gave missionaries a bad name," thank you very much! Well, let me tell you, that really made my day.

Still, one nice woman suggested I might invest my summer vacation down in Mexico and continue my college studies throughout the rest of the year. That was a little encouraging. But for the most part, I just sat there in the stands, a face in the crowd, looking out upon all these thousands of kids (most of them partway or even finished with college). And the embarrassing truth is I now feel like this teeny, tiny droplet in a great, big ocean. And I wonder what possible difference little old me can have on anything? But then again, I'm probably just tired, and I do have a cold that's making me feel kinda down too. So, I suppose it's times like this that I need to remember my verse about trusting God with all my heart.

I must admit, I'm looking forward to seeing Josh and the other guys during our trip back home. Naturally, they stayed in one of the men's dorms. (I was in the women's.) And like I said Josh mostly ignored me—okay, he completely ignored me. But I suppose that was a good thing. It did allow me to focus my attention on missions without being distracted by his great Matt Damon good looks, although I did notice a few other girls looking as well as what appeared to me to be flirting! Okay, okay, I'm not jealous. Well, not exactly. I think I'm mostly just tired and need to go home. Man, I can't wait to sleep in my own bed!

Thursday, January 3 (after a grueling trip)

Sheesh, I thought we'd never get home. A nasty snowstorm blew up shortly after we took off, and we had to go painfully slow and be careful. We took turns driving around the clock for two and a half days. Thankfully, Josh had a cell phone so we remained in touch with our families. But everyone got so tired and grumpy that I was afraid we might slide right off the road and get stuck in a snowdrift and end up just like the Donner party! Well, I doubt we actually would've turned into cannibals, but we might've killed each other off. Suffice it to say, I am quite glad to see the old homestead again. And it makes me wonder just how serious I really am about going down to Mexico to live. I mean, that's a long ways from home. Something to think about, I guess. But maybe I'll think about it tomorrow...after I've slept for about, say, nineteen or twenty hours! By the way, I don't think Josh and I exchanged more than a few sentences the entire time. Oh, well, I guess I should be thankful.

Friday, January 4 (back to the norm, whatever that is)

Even though I was kind of exhausted, it was something of a relief to be back at school today and back around kids my own age, who are just doing ordinary things like complaining about the basketball team's latest losing streak or soggy french fries in the cafeteria. Although, at the same time, it did seem slightly odd that no one here talked about saving the lost or feeding the hungry or getting Bibles to some third world tribe. And I suppose it all seems just a mite shallow in contrast to where I was only a week ago. But naturally I kept these thoughts to myself.

At least my best friends Jenny and Beanie seemed really glad to see me. And I think they were actually relieved to hear that I wasn't planning on dropping out of school my senior year and hitchhiking down to Mexico to save the world or something equally absurd. I wouldn't be surprised if they both thought I was about to go off the deep end and do something totally weird and fanatical.

But speaking of weird, here's what's got me scratching my head today. It seems that Beanie has this new "romantic interest" in her life (Joel Johnson). And this has got me a little concerned. Not so much because I thought she and Zach Streeter would ever get back together or anything, because I know they're only "just friends" now, and Josh even told me that Zach probably has a girl-friend at college. (Although I don't think Beanie knows this—or maybe she does!) But the thing is, it's been only about six months since Beanie promised God she would abstain from sex, and I suppose I sort of thought that meant she wasn't going to date either. And she hasn't. Well, until now, that is. And, of course, it's her life—and it's her decision—and I have absolutely no right to judge her. But, sheesh, this guy isn't even a Christian. And quite frankly I just don't get it!

Jenny told me that Beanie had been talking about Joel a lot last semester (and I'm wondering where was I?), and she said she wasn't a bit surprised when they finally went out—to a movie on New Year's Eve, as it turns out. But then, how could Jenny understand my concerns about Beanie? I mean, Jenny still thinks it's okay to date and stuff. I'm not even sure where she stands on the abstinence issue. And she and Trent Ziegler have been going out since before Christmas, and he's not a Christian either. But it's really none of my business, right? So why should any of it even surprise or bother me?

Maybe it's just that I'm feeling a little like the odd man out right now. You know that old fifth wheel thing. Or maybe I'm just afraid that we're all going to grow apart or that Beanie and Jenny might stop taking God seriously. Already it seems like those two are living in their own little world. I mean, they live together and work together and the fact is, I feel kind of out of it just now. So how can I possibly step in and say that I'm all worried about their spiritual conditions without sounding like a total nerd? I mean, it seems like I should be able to tell my two best friends how I feel, but I'm not so sure. What if they see me as some kind of religious fanatic? (Am I a fanatic?)

Oh, maybe I'm just overreacting to what is simply normal high school behavior. To be perfectly honest, I feel pretty confused right now and I'm thinking I better just pray about all this stuff and try really hard to keep my big mouth shut before I'm really sorry. (Now, wouldn't that be a good exercise in self-control!)

DEAR GOD, PLEASE HELP ME NOT TO COME DOWN ON MY FRIENDS (OR ANYONE ELSE FOR THAT MATTER). AND HELP ME NOT TO LET THEIR CHOICES INFLUENCE MY DECISIONS. I KNOW HOW YOU'VE ASKED ME TO LIVE AND I DON'T WANT TO COMPROMISE. I WANT TO STAY STRONG FOR YOU. AMEN.

two

Sunday, January 6 (sigh of relief)

I spent the night at my grandma's house last night (where Beanie and Jenny are living until Grandma comes back from snowbirding down in Arizona). And it felt just like old times with the three of us hanging out together. Believe it or not, we actually made popcorn and chocolate chip cookies. Talk about pigging out! It was Beanie's idea, really, since this is one part of childhood that she seriously missed out on living with her less-than-traditional mom, Lynn. But I have to confess that Jenny and I kinda liked it too. We kept calling ourselves the three old maids, although I think that's hardly likely! Especially with Jenny who gets asked out several times a week (according to Beanie who fields half the phone calls). Have I ever mentioned that Jenny looks a lot like Catherine Zeta-Jones (only a younger, thinner version)? Well, Jenny says that's absolutely crazy, but I'm not the first one who's noticed. Anyway, I'm sure those two were just saying the old maid thing for my benefit since they figure that's my major goal in life. Ha! Then we sat down with our carb feast and watched these goofy old movies from my grandma's funky video collection.

We stayed up until about three in the morning watching Seven Brides for Seven Brothers. Talk about corny! Then we still managed to get up in time to go to youth group and church. After that we invited Andrea LeMarsh to come to the mall with us. We got some lunch and then shopped the after-Christmas sales, which are pretty picked over by now, although Beanie did manage to find a jacket that we all thought looked very cool on her. (And to think it wasn't even from a secondhand store!) Then Jenny found a pair of boots she'd been wanting that were marked way down. So those two were pretty delirious. Andrea and I didn't have such great luck (a good thing since I'm still fairly broke after the missions conference). Anyway, we tried on funny hats and ugly purses and generally acted childish and immature. But I must say it felt pretty good.

And so now I'm thinking all my previous worries about Jenny and Beanie falling away from God were just some kind of neurotic paranoia on my part. And after hearing them share today in youth group—they both responded to Greg's question about who should come first in our lives—I'm sure they're both doing just fine in that regard. Chalk it up to another Caitlin O'Conner lesson on judging others and why it's not a terribly smart thing to do.

Tuesday, January 8 (foot-in-mouth disease strikes again)

Well, I've gone and done it now. Once again, I've managed
to totally alienate my oldest and best friend. I really
stuck my foot in it when Jenny and Beanie and I went to
the basketball game tonight. It was Beanie's idea to go,
of course, since Joel plays center for the team (which is
not having such a great season). I don't know why it didn't
occur to me earlier that he was the one behind Beanie's
recent interest in basketball. (I mean, she used to think
that sport was only slightly less absurd than football.)
Anyway, I thought going to the game sounded fun and I
even offered to drive. I tried not to notice when Beanie
was yelling like a wild woman for Joel to score—I mean, we
were all cheering for the team (and they only lost by one
point!). But after the game, Beanie said we could go on
without her, that she'd catch a ride home with Joel.

"But why do you want to do that?" I asked (somewhat
stupidly, I can see now in retrospect).

Beanie frowned. "Why not?"

"Well, I don't know, Beanie. I guess it just doesn't seem
right to me." I'm sure I kind of stumbled over my words at
that point, and I know I probably sounded just like an old
mother hen. What I really wanted to say was how I was
seriously worried about her getting involved with another
guy again. (I mean, it seems like she's barely gotten over
Zach.) But how do you say something like that to your
friend with a bunch of people hanging around?

But it was too late. I watched Beanie's eyebrows come together in a dark <u>V</u>, and when her nostrils flared I knew I was in trouble. Somehow I'd stepped over the line. Although I wasn't quite sure how.

"Caitlin O'Conner!" She spat out my name, her lips puckered as if it tasted like dirt. Then she took a deep breath (like she was trying to control her temper) and just slowly shook her head. She looked like she was about to correct someone the age of my little cousin Oliver when she finally spoke. "You know, I think you're prejudiced."

Now, I forgot to mention that Beanie's new heartthrob (Joel Johnson) is black (or African-American or whatever the politically correct term is these days). Actually his skin is sort of a nice caramel color and he's really good looking, but I'm getting away from the point here. The thing is: I am NOT, nor have I EVER been prejudiced—against anyone! At least not based on skin color or ethnicity. I mean, I may have been slightly prejudiced against snooty popular kids once (way back before Jenny and I became friends). But I don't believe I've ever been prejudiced against someone simply because their skin, hair, or eye color was different than mine. I mean, that's ridiculous. And for Beanie to say that to me (and in public) was incredibly offensive. And I was actually speechless for a few seconds. Then finally I gathered my wits and looked her right in the eyes. "I am <u>not</u> prejudiced!" I sputtered. "I'm—I'm just worried about you—"

"Worried about what?" Now her words grew loud

enough to turn a few more heads (as if enough weren't looking already), but I sensed she no longer cared if she made a great big scene (remember Beanie likes theatrics). Then she put her face up close to mine and peered at me like she was trying to see right inside of my brain, like she thought I was hiding something deep and dark and sinister in there.

At about that point, I started feeling pretty lame, not to mention awfully conspicuous. And I felt fairly certain that everyone within earshot was listening now, not to mention staring (or so it seemed at the time).

"Come on, you guys," urged Jenny, but I could hear her nervous laugh. "Just chill, okay?"

Still I wasn't ready to let this thing go. (I hate being unjustly accused, especially in public.) "But you don't understand, Beanie, I just—"

"Caitlin." Beanie's voice grew quieter now, but her dark eyes flashed at me—like a warning sign. "Drop it, okay?"

Jenny tugged on my arm. "Come on, Caitlin. Let's go now." She winked at Beanie. "Don't worry, I'll handle this."

Beanie just rolled her eyes, then shrugged. "Yeah, see ya later."

Without saying another word, I fumed all the way across the parking lot. I felt humiliated and completely misunderstood. And I'm sure being misunderstood is what bugged me the most. I absolutely HATE being misunderstood!

"Whew!" Jenny closed the car door and sighed. "Glad

that's over with. What's gotten into you, Caitlin?"

I turned and stared at her. "Me?"

"Yeah, you were acting—uh, shall we say, slightly nuts."

I groaned and leaned back into the seat. "You don't understand. I'm just concerned about Beanie."

"Yeah?" She threw me a suspicious glance from the corner of her eye. "And why exactly is that?"

And then we went round and round, this time with me trying to explain how I didn't want to see Beanie getting hurt again. And how I felt like dating just invites trouble. And suddenly I had Jenny all over me like a bad case of zits, and now she was getting all defensive.

"Caitlin O'Conner, you can't expect everyone to give up dating just because you did. And, besides, we all know you still spend time with Josh. Sheesh, you guys went off to that conference together for a whole week. I mean, what's up with that? Talk about dating!"

"We are not dating!"

"But you guys still like each other, don't you?"

Suddenly I remembered how Jenny and Josh had been dating (seriously dating) less than a year ago— before I'd come between them. And I remembered how it seemed like she hated me then. I also remembered the jealousy I'd felt when she and Josh got back together again. And suddenly I felt so completely confused that I couldn't even think straight, let alone talk sensibly. So I just drove her home in silence. But when I stopped my car I felt like I needed to say something. "Jenny, I'm sorry. I know I'm not doing a very good job of explaining how I feel right now. And I know I probably sound pretty stupid. But the thing is, I just don't want to see Beanie or you getting hurt because of guys."

Jenny threw back her head and laughed. "Caitlin, you worry way too much. Don't you understand that we've all got to live our own lives and make our own mistakes?"

I nodded. "Yeah, I know you're right."

"And even if Beanie and I haven't kissed dating goodbye, like you claim to have done, we still might be smarter than you give us credit for."

"Yeah, yeah." I forced a smile. "I know I must've sounded like a total idiot tonight."

"It's okay, Caitlin. I forgive you, and I'm sure Beanie will too—in time. Besides, it's a good reminder to all of us that you're not so perfect after all." She made a smirky face then gently punched me in the arm.

"Hey, I never said I was perfect!"

"It's not always what you say, Sister Caitlin."

I shut my mouth and just nodded. As much as it hurt, I knew she was probably right. I probably do come across as (gag!) little "Miss Perfect." And, man oh man, I totally HATE that!

DEAR GOD, WHAT IS WRONG WITH ME? WHERE DO I GET OFF ACTING LIKE I KNOW IT ALL? I HATE THAT I MIGHT BE COMING ACROSS AS PERFECT OR SUPERIOR. WHO DO I THINK I AM? OH, PLEASE,

PLEASE HELP ME TO BE HUMBLE AND NONJUDGMEN-
TAL. HELP ME TO BE MORE LIKE YOU. AND, PLEASE,
FORGIVE ME FOR BLOWING IT SO BADLY. AMEN.

Thursday, January 10 (who am I?)

Somehow Beanie and I have sort of patched things up
this week, but she still acts like she has this sneaking suspicion that I might really be a little bit prejudiced. Which
I must admit really irks me!

"Caitlin, it's only natural," she said to me at lunchtime
today. "Everyone is prejudiced about one thing or
another."

"But I really, truly don't think I am."

She shook her head. "Yeah, but what if you're just in
denial?"

Jenny groaned. "Oh, pleeease, don't you two start this
up again."

"What about Jenny," I continued. "Is she prejudiced
too?"

"Sure," said Jenny lightly. "I'll be the first one to
admit that I probably wouldn't go out with an ugly
boy."

"What if he was really sweet and smart?" I coun-
tered.

She shrugged. "I'm sorry. Call me superficial, shallow,
trivial—whatever, but I happen to like cute boys." She
nodded toward the doorway. "Like Trent there." Then
she waved and took off to join him.

I sighed. "So, does _that_ count as prejudice?"

Beanie nodded. "Yep. But at least she's honest about it."

"Okay. I suppose I am prejudiced about some things. But not skin color, Beanie. Really."

"You don't have any friends of color."

"Maybe not close ones, but I consider Anna Parker to be a friend. I've known her since grade school and I've always been friendly to her."

"Did you ever invite her to your house?"

"No. But you know how I used to be kind of shy. I mean, for years I never invited hardly anyone over—except for you, Beanie. And come to think of it, you happen to be Jewish, by the way. And I was never prejudiced against that. Was I?" For once I felt I was getting the upper hand again.

"Ah, yes." She raised her forefinger as if to make a critical point. "But then again, you did manage to convert me, didn't you?"

"Beanie!" I stared at her with disbelief.

Then she started laughing. "Had you going, didn't I?"

Well, she did have me going. And in some ways I'm starting to think maybe she's right. Maybe I AM prejudiced, but I'm just too oblivious to know it. And that scares me! So now I'm really praying that God will show me what's inside me (okay, not everything—that'd be way too horrifying). But if I really am prejudiced, I want to know about it ASAP. And then I want to do something to change.

DEAR GOD, I KNOW YOU KNOW MY HEART. I MEAN, YOU KNOW ME BETTER THAN I KNOW ME. SO

PLEASE SHOW ME IF I'M PREJUDICED AND THEN
HELP ME TO DEAL WITH IT. I WANT TO LOVE EVERY-
ONE THE WAY YOU LOVE THEM—UNCONDITIONALLY!
THANK YOU FOR LOVING ME EVEN WHEN I'M ACTING
LIKE A TOTAL JERK. AMEN.

THREE

Friday, January 11 (more confusion)

To try and make up for my recent embarrassing fiasco at the last basketball game, I offered to drive Beanie and Jenny to the away game tonight (about an hour's drive). Jenny had to work but begged us to stop by Pizza Hut after the game to keep her company. For the most part, things went much better tonight. Not only that but our team actually won! Afterward we did go out for pizza to celebrate (which pleased Jenny). Trent came with us too. And I didn't even blow it by saying something totally lame when I noticed how he and Jenny got all kissy-faced back in the hallway by the bathrooms (when they thought nobody was looking, of course).

Then later on Joel and some of his friends joined us for pizza, and it was pretty cool just hanging with these guys that I normally don't spend much time with at school. And I guess I understand why Beanie likes Joel so much. It's easy to see he's a lot more than just a jock. He's really smart and funny and always has something interesting to say. Still it bothers me that he's not a Christian. But I never let on about any of this while we were at the pizza joint. I just laughed and joked around and acted like one of the crowd (even though I sort of felt like an outsider—now why is that???).

It's too bad I didn't continue my little routine for the rest of the evening. But unfortunately, I just couldn't keep my mouth shut later on when I drove Beanie and Jenny home.

"Okay, now forgive me for beating a dead horse here, but I've just got to know something," I began when we were about five minutes from their house. (In hindsight I have to admit I knew this was a mistake, but I just blundered on anyway.) "Are you guys honestly telling me that you're really not the least bit concerned that the boys you're dating aren't even Christians?"

"Oh, no," groaned Jenny. "Here comes another dating sermon."

Beanie raised her hands dramatically. "Please, Sister Caitlin, can't you just give it a rest tonight? Like chill?"

"Look, you guys, I'm really not trying to be preachy. But I just don't get it. Do you honestly think it's okay to go out with boys who aren't Christians?"

Now for no apparent reason Jenny started giggling, and irritatingly enough Beanie started laughing too. It's like they were getting each other all worked up and hysterical over something that I frankly just didn't get. And I felt stupid and totally out of it. I mean, I had absolutely no idea what was so funny, and so naturally I assumed they were laughing at me. Like who wouldn't? So, of course, I got a little offended.

"What's so funny?" I finally asked in an uptight voice as I pulled into their driveway.

"I don't know," said Beanie lightly. "I'm just laughing because she's laughing." And of course this sent Jenny into a whole new round of spasms.

"Oh, I don't know. It's just that you're so worried—" sputtered Jenny. "I mean, you're sitting here getting all freaked about what'll happen if we date guys who aren't Christians." Laugh-chortle-snort-snort! "But just think about it, Cate, we both already dated boys who were Christians—" she exploded hysterically again. "And, I mean, look where that got us!"

Now Beanie was totally losing it again too, like she finally got the joke. "Yeah, Caitlin, doncha remember, girl-friend? I got myself knocked up with a good ol' Christian boy!"

Jenny hooted now. "And I lost my virginity with another!"

I felt pretty stupid just then. And the two of them were laughing so hard that tears were actually stream-ing down their faces.

"Come on, you guys," I tried. "You sound like you don't even care—"

Beanie turned and looked at me with tears still wet

on her cheeks. "Hey, we know we've made some pretty big mistakes, Caitlin. Do you really think we want to go back there again?"

"Yeah, and it's cool that your life is so perfectly on track," began Jenny, trying hard to regain her composure now.

"I didn't say—"

"But can't you see..." she continued, "that dating Christian guys isn't exactly a foolproof plan either?"

I sighed and just shook my head. I mean, to be perfectly honest, I knew they were both partially right. After all, I've had my hardest lessons with a Christian boy too (same one as Jenny, come to think of it). "Well, maybe that's why dating isn't such a good idea," I tried to say gently—sort of tentative-like. I really did NOT want to come across as preachy again.

"Look, Cate, if it works for you, fine," said Beanie as she wiped her eyes. "But it's really unfair for you to put your standards on us. Besides, I think I learned a lot when I dated Zach. Honestly, I don't think I'll ever be that stupid again."

"Me neither!" exclaimed Jenny. And then the two exchanged high fives, like that settled it.

"But then why even bother—"

Beanie cut me off. "We've got to live our own lives, Caitlin. Don't you get it? If you want to avoid the dating game, that's your business and we won't push you to date. Okay? But you just can't keep going around and telling everyone else how to live."

"I don't tell everyone—"

"No, you usually save it all up for us," said Jenny.

"Yeah, it makes us feel so special." Beanie's sarcasm cut right through me. And I knew they were right and I was wrong.

"Yeah, yeah, I know." I gave in, feeling like a total idiot again. "I'm sorry, you guys. It's just that I really care about you and—"

"It's okay," said Jenny. "We know you do. But just don't worry so much, okay? And who knows, maybe God will use us to reach these poor, heathen guys."

Beanie started giggling again, then quickly sobered when Jenny tossed her a warning glance. "Yeah, Jenny could be right," she said. "I mean, I haven't hid anything about what I believe from Joel. Right from the start I told him all about how I became a Christian and how important that is to me. And I really think he respects that."

"And Trent does too. And you know he's even come to church a couple times."

"Yeah, but he still says he's an atheist."

"Oh, Cate," complained Jenny. "So did I not that long ago."

"I suppose you're right. I guess I'm just being too judgmental—again."

"No big deal, Caitlin," said Beanie in a placating tone. "We're used to you by now. And we love you anyway."

"Thanks," I said, feeling pretty lame.

And so when I got home tonight, I still felt a little confused. I mean, I feel so strongly that I'm not supposed to date. And the primary reason is because I know how easy it is (when you're in an intimate relationship) to get in over your head (and it can happen fast). At the very least you can get hurt, or else you can get pressured into things you wouldn't normally do (like having sex—or even just seriously making out, which can still make you feel like crud afterward). And so, to me, it just makes more sense not to get into that situation in the first place. Besides that, I truly believe that's what God has told me to do.

But when I talk to Beanie and Jenny about this stuff, I really start wondering if I'm all wet. I mean, what they say does makes sense, well, sort of. Although I seriously doubt that dating is going to get the guys interested in God. In fact, I'm sure it could backfire right in Beanie's and Jenny's faces. I remember not that long ago when I was getting interested in God and Josh proved to be nothing more than a great big and somewhat devastating distraction for me.

But just the same, it never fails that every time I try to talk to Beanie and Jenny about any of this, I come out sounding like this totally freaked-out and paranoid church-nerd. And I really don't like that image much. But at the same time I will NOT compromise my own convictions either. I just wish this dating thing wasn't so confusing—or volatile.

DEAR GOD, PLEASE SHOW ME WHAT I'M SUPPOSED TO DO HERE. I REALLY BELIEVE YOU'VE MADE IT

CLEAR THAT DATING ISN'T FOR ME. BUT WHAT I
DON'T UNDERSTAND IS WHY IT'S NOT LIKE THAT
FOR EVERYONE ELSE TOO. I MEAN, IT JUST SEEMS
LIKE IT SHOULD ALL BE CLEAR-CUT, BLACK AND
WHITE, RIGHT OR WRONG. BUT MAYBE IT'S NOT
ALWAYS LIKE THAT. CAN YOU PLEASE SHED SOME
LIGHT ON THIS FOR ME? BECAUSE, REALLY, I WANT
WHAT YOU WANT!!! AND I DON'T WANT TO KEEP
ALIENATING MY FRIENDS. HELP ME. AMEN

Sunday, January 13 (a ray of hope)
To my complete surprise (and Beanie's triumph!) Joel
Johnson came to youth group and church today. Beanie
told me that she'd purposely invited him after our conversation the other night (just to show me, I suppose!). But
it was a smart move on her part, and I really think everyone there made him feel pretty welcome. He even asked
a couple of very insightful questions during youth group
(which Greg handled brilliantly). Then afterward a
bunch of us stood around in the parking lot together, just
joking and talking before Beanie and Jenny had to go to
work at Pizza Hut.

"Yeah, you guys have a pretty nice church—for
white folks, that is." Then Joel laughed and added, "Uh,
maybe you guys didn't notice, but I kind of stuck out in
there."

"You mean because you're so tall?" teased Jenny.

He grinned. "No, I mean because you guys are such
palefaces."

And that's when it occurred to me that other than a Vietnamese family and a Hispanic couple, our church is primarily white. But I had to wonder why I'd never really noticed that before. Maybe Beanie was right about me.

"But don't feel too bad," said Joel. "The church where my mom and sister go is no different. I seriously doubt that a white person has ever set foot past their doors."

"Why is that?" asked Beanie with a very intense look.

"It's called segregation. And it's just the way it's always been." Joel laughed lightly. Although judging by his expression, I didn't think he really thought it was all that funny. Then he continued. "And I guess we shouldn't get too bent out of shape because in actuality, it's been a whole lot worse than this in the past. I guess we've progressed a little in the last few decades." He grinned. "So, is that enough black history for you folks, or would you like to sign up for my night class—African-American History 101?"

"But I thought we were integrated now," said Jenny. "I mean, didn't we get desegregated in the sixties? Isn't that what that bussing thing was all about?"

Joel shook his head and rolled his eyes like he was talking to a bunch of preschoolers. "Well, you can force some kinds of change, like piling kids into buses and forcing them to go miles across town to a school where they don't know anybody and nobody really wants them there anyway. But real change, lasting change, has got to come from the heart."

I blinked. I knew Joel was deep, but I was pretty impressed. "But I still don't get it, Joel," I said. "Don't you think that most kids at our school don't have a problem with racial issues? Don't you think we're all fairly color blind?"

Joel laughed. "You better look again, Caitlin."

"What do you mean?"

"Haven't you noticed how cliques, for the most part, are pretty much color coded, or in other words segregated—either by race or economics or whatever? For the most part, there's not a whole lot of mixing up going on."

I tried to imagine the lunchroom for a moment. "Yeah, I suppose you're right. I guess I never quite saw it that way. But what about when we all met for pizza the other night? That was cool, wasn't it?"

He smiled. "Yeah, now that might've been a little closer to color blind." He laughed again. "If there really is such a thing."

"Well, it's too bad we don't all just mix it up all the time," said Jenny.

Beanie grabbed Joel's hand and swung it in the air. "Hey, I'm all for mixing it up. How about you, Joel?"

He grinned down on her. "Count me in, babe!"

I glanced at him, not too sure how comfortable I was with <u>that</u> kind of mixing it up (or was I just being judgmental again?). "Well, maybe we can do something to mix it up more at school too," I suggested (trying to repress my dating concerns about Beanie). "How about if we all start hanging out together more during lunch and stuff."

"Works for me," said Joel. "But I can't make any promises for the rest of my buddies."

"Well, I think it seems like what Jesus would expect from us," I added, hoping it didn't sound like I was about to give them all another sermon. Because I really meant it!

"Yeah," agreed Joel. "I might not be a Christian, not like you guys are anyway, but I think God made us all different for some pretty smart reasons. Mostly I think he just wants us to learn to accept and love others for who they are."

"Preach it, brother!" said Beanie.

"Amen!" I added, then we all laughed.

And so, it'll be interesting to see what comes of this "mixing it up" tomorrow. I really do think it's what Jesus would do. We've learned about a lot of these issues in school, and "racial reconciliation" is a popular term in social science classes, but it never seems to really leak out into the hallways and the cafeteria. But I'm thinking it's like Joel said. Until people really change in their hearts, nothing will ever really change for good.

DEAR GOD, PLEASE HELP ME TO CHANGE FROM MY HEART. I DON'T THINK I LOOK DOWN ON PEOPLE OF DIFFERENT RACES OR WHATEVER. BUT MAYBE I JUST NEED TO REACH OUT MORE TO OTHERS. HELP ME TO SEE PEOPLE THE WAY YOU SEE THEM. HELP ME TO LOVE OTHERS THE WAY YOU DO— REGARDLESS OF DIFFERENCES. AMEN.

Wednesday, January 16 (growing up is hard
to do)

I don't know if it's just the January blahs or me or whatever, but this sure has been a trying couple of weeks for
me. I think the only encouraging thing has been the e-mail
I've received from Josh. Well, that and knowing that God
still loves me despite what a fool I seem to make of
myself on a disturbingly regular basis.

Beanie told me (and loudly too) that I was a prude
today. Well, that was after I made a snide remark
about her and Joel kissing in public. I know, I know. I have
no business making comments like that. And at this rate
they'll be calling me "Mother Superior" in no time. (Oh, I
sure hope they don't think of that one—Sister Caitlin is
bad enough.) But to be called a prude by my best
friend, right there in the Harrison High cafeteria, was a
bit much, if you ask me. Just the same, I probably had it
coming. But what made me feel even worse than
Beanie's name-calling was the expression in Joel's eyes—
like I had personally hurt him. And I almost apologized, but
then I was afraid it would seem patronizing because in a
way we were all just joking around. At least I thought we
were joking. But to be perfectly honest, my feelings did
get hurt. So why shouldn't his have been hurt as well?

Oh, man, sometimes life feels so complicated. And I
can't help but remember when I was just a kid and my
biggest problem was whether my socks went with my dress
or that my little brother was being a pain. Not that Ben's

still not a pain sometimes, but he's really growing up fast, and I find I'm liking him more as a person now. Well, most of the time anyway—not when he's pounding on the bathroom door and telling me to "beat cheeks outta there."

But back to my one encouraging bright spot these days. Josh's e-mails have been so great lately. I really opened up to him, telling him all about my struggles with this nondating thing. (Since it seems like I don't have anyone else I can talk to, besides God, that is.) Anyway, I explained how Beanie and Jenny are always on my case (or maybe I'm on theirs). But Josh really seems to understand how I feel, and he always has something helpful to say.

Like the other day I told him how I couldn't understand why God would tell me not to do something (like dating, for instance), but that it would be perfectly okay for everyone else. (I mean, it doesn't seem fair.) Then Josh wrote back and reminded me about what Clay used to say. Just thinking about Clay made me miss him more than ever, and suddenly I wondered what life would be like if he'd never been shot last year.... Anyway, Josh reminded me how Clay always made a point to say that "convictions are very personal" and "what God tells you to do is for <u>you and you alone</u>."

Then Josh wrote about when Peter (the outspoken apostle guy) had this dream or vision or whatever about eating all this food that was considered unfit to eat by Jewish people. And Peter was kind of repulsed by the idea of eating those things (like snakes and snails...and I can't

really blame him there—yuck!), but God told him in the
dream that it was okay. So Peter went ahead and ate
that weird food. (I don't think it was really snakes and
snails, but maybe some pork or shrimp or something non-
kosher.) But the thing was: He ate it with people who
weren't Jewish, and as a result they got saved.

Josh's whole point in sharing this with me had to do
with Beanie and Jenny. He said that maybe what
they've doing really is okay—for them, that is. Maybe
their faith is stronger than mine and God will actually
use them to reach out to Joel and Trent. Well, I'm still not
sure how I feel about that. But then, Josh reminded me
that I shouldn't judge others. Duh! You'd think I'd have
figured that one out by now, but I guess I still need a few
reminders. So anyway, his words were hard to hear but
pretty encouraging. And I e-mailed him back and asked
Josh if he'd ever considered being a preacher or a
teacher because what he'd shared with me came
across really clear and understandable. And guess
what? He said he's actually been praying about it.
Amazing!

Now, like I said, this communication with Josh has been
the bright spot in my drab little life lately. But now even
that has me concerned. Okay, I know I'm taking a risk of
sounding really neurotic now, but isn't that what diaries
are for—to express our darkest, deepest fears and all
that? But now I'm feeling worried about what Jenny said
about me and Josh, about how my relationship with him
sort of proves that I never really gave up dating at all.

Yikes! But then again it's not like we're really dating. Not really. Or are we? Because I hate the thought that I could be playing the hypocrite here. I mean, we're just e-mailing each other. And it's not like that's tempting me to have sex or taking something away from my relationship with God. So why do I all of the sudden feel guilty? To be perfectly gut-level honest, it's almost as if there's this thing inside me that keeps saying, "You have to be perfect, Caitlin O'Conner. You have to be perfect." But what's up with that? Is it me? Is it God? Or am I just going totally nuts???

DEAR GOD, BEANIE AND JENNY SAY I WORRY TOO MUCH. AND I'M STARTING TO WONDER IF MAYBE THEY'RE RIGHT. IT'S LIKE I KEEP WANTING TO BE BETTER AND BETTER FOR YOU, BUT THE WHOLE WHILE I SEEM TO BE GETTING WORSE AND WORSE. IT'S LIKE I DON'T EVEN KNOW WHO I AM ANYMORE. CAN YOU PLEASE HELP ME OUT HERE? AMEN.

FOUR

Thursday, January 17 (some relief)

My Aunt Steph and her husband Tony
(who's also our pastor) came over to our house for dinner
tonight (naturally they brought little Oliver too). And
afterward I went to clean up in the kitchen, and Tony
very graciously offered to help. While we were filling the
dishwasher, he asked if everything was going okay with
me. Then he mentioned that I seemed more quiet and
reserved than usual. And, man, that did it. I just started
spilling my guts to the poor unsuspecting man. Being a pastor, I suppose he's used to that kind of thing, but I must
admit I felt a little embarrassed at first. Just the same
I told him how I feel guilty about a lot of things, how I
worry about Beanie and Jenny and the kids in Mexico,
and about my relationship with Josh—and well, just about
everything. And Tony didn't even think I was crazy. He
said I have a very sensitive spirit and that it would
always be very important for me to keep my relationship

with God as close and tight as possible, because the more I trust God, the more I will relax and have peace. He also encouraged me to read my Bible more.

"My brother Clay was a lot like that after he got saved," he explained as he applied some elbow grease to the stubborn lasagna dish. "It's like he had this really tight connection with God that made him wise beyond his years. But as a result he had to be real careful about how he talked to others because it sometimes made him seem judgmental or superior. We used to talk about stuff like this for hours at a time. But I think he was really getting a handle on it. Even shortly before he died, I remember him telling me he was worried that he was coming across as judgmental with the youth group, and that troubled him a lot."

"Yes!" I cried. "That's it. I keep feeling like I'm judging everyone. And it's driving me bonkers."

He laughed. "Well, just remember how Jesus warned us again and again about not judging each other. And what is right for one person isn't necessarily right for another. God deals with us all on an individual basis."

"Yeah, that's almost exactly what Josh e-mailed to me."

"Looks like God's trying to tell you something, Caitlin."

We talked a while longer, and then I changed the subject and told him about what we were doing at school (our little racial reconciliation project).

"That's great, Caitlin."

"Well, it wasn't really my idea. Beanie and Joel are kind of the instigators."

"You know, I've been praying about ways to get the church more integrated." Tony wiped his hands on a dish towel and thought for a moment. "Maybe this is the beginning of something."

"It's been kind of interesting at school. We've gotten some strange looks from some kids. But we've also seen others starting to do the same thing as us. Or at least it seems that way. It's like some of those old barriers are coming down. Not to make it sound like we haven't had any opposition, because we definitely have. There's this one girl named Natala who thought I was making a move on her boyfriend, Jamal, which I wasn't. But anyway when I took the time to explain to her how we just wanted to make more friends, she lightened up a little. I just wish we could do something more."

Then Tony looked as if some sort of light had just gone on inside his brain. "Hey, maybe you guys would like to have some kind of get-together or something at the church."

"Like a party or something?"

"Yeah, some sort of social gathering that gives you a place to get to know each other besides school, but a place that doesn't have any other—uh, well, negative factors interfering."

"You mean like alcohol or drugs?"

He nodded. "Believe me, I know what it's like out there. It's not all that long ago since Clay was into that stuff." His face grew sad.

I sighed. "Yeah, that must've been hard." But what I was really thinking was how Tony must still miss his little brother a lot. I know I still do. Just the same, I couldn't think of anything to say that hasn't already been said. Maybe it's just one of those things that takes a lot of time to get over.

"Hey, you two," called Stephie. "Oliver is getting pretty sleepy out here, and he has to get up for nursery school in the morning."

Tony walked over and put his arm around her. "Yeah, sweetie, I was just thinking the same thing."

I stared at the two of them for a moment and thought once again how totally amazing it is that God brought them together. They are so totally perfect for each other. But if you think about it, just a couple years ago you'd never have guessed something like that would've been possible. I mean, Stephie's life was kind of a mess and Tony was this dedicated pastor. Who ever would've thought they'd end up together? But I guess God is bigger than what we can think or dream or even imagine. And I suppose that's one more reason He doesn't want us to judge anyone or anything. We just don't have all the right information. But He does! And knowing that makes me feel a whole lot better. Hopefully, I'm starting to get it. On the other hand, just when I think I understand something, I usually fall flat on my face. So look out below!

Friday, January 18 (the plan)
Just this morning, I told Beanie about how Tony had suggested having a get-together at church.

"How about tomorrow night?" she suggested.

"Tomorrow? Why so soon?"

"We could call it a Martin Luther King, Jr. party."

"Oh yeah," I said. "That's right. But do you think we could get it together by then?"

"Well, how much do we have to get together? Just round up some food and stuff, then open the doors, right?"

I had to grin. Leave it to Beanie to boil everything down to pure simplicity. It's just her style, and I have to admire her for it. "Okay, then. I'll call Tony and see if it works." And I remembered to pray about it on my way to the pay phone. (Unfortunately for me, I do not carry a cell phone or a beeper, as do so many kids these days. I keep telling Dad that I'm electronically impaired, but he doesn't seem to take it too seriously.)

As it turned out, Tony thought it was a totally brilliant idea. (Again I had to give the credit to Beanie, but I didn't mind.) And so it was all set, and at lunchtime we found Jenny and the three of us started inviting everyone we could think of to come. (We figured only a small percentage would show anyway.) Some of the kids kind of made fun of us (having "a church party?"), but we just took it all in stride. And before long Joel was getting all involved too, and he got kids to agree to bring food and stuff. Suddenly this little get-together was taking on a life of its own.

"What do you think we'll do to pass the time?" I asked when we finally sat down to eat our lunch.

"Maybe we should have a little planning session," suggested Jenny.

Beanie turned to Joel. "Maybe you should be in charge."

Now I wasn't too sure about that. I mean, Joel himself freely admits that he's not a Christian. And it might be kind of weird to have him leading this thing (at our church) when he's not even saved. But (now hold on to your hat!) I wisely kept these slightly judgmental thoughts to myself. You see, I am learning. And so it was settled; Joel would be in charge.

"Is that too much for you to deal with?" I asked him. "I mean, I know you have a ball game tonight, and then—"

He waved his hand. "No problem."

Saturday, January 19 (our Martin Luther King, Jr. party)

The big night came and I'd like to say the whole thing went off without a single hitch. And it did, mostly. First off, it seemed slightly miraculous that both Beanie and Jenny could get off work early to come. And then we were totally blown away by the crowd—Jenny said she counted over a hundred! And a real mix too. Joel, as promised, handled the agenda. He brought his boom box and a good collection of CDs (all black musicians, of course), and he played everything from blues to jazz to rap. And when some of his friends tried to sneak some vodka into the punch bowl, he stepped right in and reminded them they were in a church and if they needed to get drunk, they'd have to go do it somewhere else. Then when some of the Hispanic guys started getting into it with some of the black guys, once again Joel stepped in (this time with the help of some of his basketball buddies), and they amazingly talked these guys out of fighting. But it was a tense moment, believe me, and the room got kind of quiet except for the boom box, which was playing an old Chubby Checker song just then.

But Joel used this opportunity to get everyone's attention, and he grabbed the microphone and read (in a really dramatic voice) Dr. Martin Luther King, Jr.'s "I Have a Dream" speech. And, man, was the crowd ever quiet. It was totally awesome! After he finished he said a few words about how far we'd come since the good reverend made this speech back in the sixties, but how far we still had to go. Then he encouraged everyone to just keep visiting and have a good time. And so we did.

It sure might seem like a pretty small step in the big scheme of things, but I think Dr. King would've been proud. And I'm sure that God was pleased with us because I know we're all God's children, and He wants us to love our brothers and sisters—which brings me to my latest revelation. Are you ready for this? Well, I'm thinking, okay, if we're all God's children, then that makes every single one of us brothers and sisters (whether we've saved or not). Because God loves us all long before we ever get saved, so why shouldn't we do the same? Now, I'm not saying that I'm all resolved over Jenny and Beanie dating guys who aren't Christians, but at least I'm thinking of Trent and Joel as my brothers now (even if they aren't saved—yet!). And let me tell you that's pretty cool.

We ended the evening by singing "Jesus Loves the Little Children." Okay, this was my idea (and at first I felt a little dorky for suggesting a kid's song), but it was really cool when everyone joined in—some people even held hands! And then we stood around and visited for a while longer and some kids asked why we couldn't do something like this on a regular basis. So Beanie's going to call up Pastor Tony and find out. And I'm sure he'll think it's a great idea.

THANK YOU, GOD, FOR WHAT HAPPENED TONIGHT! AND NOW I PRAY THAT ALL MY BROTHERS AND SISTERS WILL COME TO KNOW YOU THE WAY I DO— AND GIVE THEIR HEARTS TO YOU. AND I ASK YOU TO HELP ME WHEN I TALK TO THEM, HELP ME TO BE A LIGHT WHO SHINES FOR YOU. I KNOW YOU'VE CALLED ME TO BE A MISSIONARY AND I KNOW THAT DOESN'T MEAN I HAVE TO TRAVEL A THOUSAND MILES TO DO IT. PLEASE, GOD, USE ME RIGHT HERE—RIGHT WHERE I LIVE—RIGHT WHERE I GO TO SCHOOL. AMEN!

Tuesday, January 22 (following up)

School has been totally amazing so far this week. I mean, it's like something really big has happened. There's this cool sense of unity and friendship and trust. Okay, it's not with everyone. But a lot of kids (mainly those who went to the party) are acting different. I even ate lunch with Anna Parker today, and she asked me what started this whole thing. I told her I thought it was mostly a God thing, and then I told her about my relationship with Jesus. And she told me that she'd accepted Christ at a church day camp when she was six years old, but that she'd kind of forgotten about it after a few years. Now she never goes to church anymore, although she said she still tries to do what's right and doesn't necessarily see herself as a bad person. So anyway, I invited her to come to church with me and even offered to pick her up. For some reason she seemed kind of suspicious just then, but she said she'd think about it, and I'm praying she'll say yes.

But lots of other cool things are happening too. Beanie and Jenny have told me neat things about people they've been talking to. And Beanie said that Tony thought it would be great for us to keep using the church as a gathering place, but he suggested that we get our youth pastor involved. And I think that's a good idea. So Beanie suggested that Greg and Joel might want to get together (which is a brilliant idea—Beanie sometimes amazes me!). I just know God is up to something big at Harrison High.

Not only that, but we all sat together during the basketball game tonight. And when our team won, we all went totally nuts (breaking out of a losing streak does that to you). And, let me tell you, it was just really cool! It's like I've never had so many friends before. And whenever I get worried that some (probably most) of these kids aren't Christians, I just remind myself that they are all God's kids (my brothers and sisters) and that I get to love them, and talk to them, and keep praying that they'll all get saved—sooner or later! Because the closer I get to some of these kids, the more I can see how much they really need Jesus. And then I remember how just ONE YEAR ago I was in the same boat they are. Wow, that really blows my mind. And when I think of how much God has done in my life in such a short time, I'm just amazed. Totally amazed!

DEAR GOD, WHATEVER IS HAPPENING HERE IN OUR SCHOOL, I JUST ASK THAT YOU KEEP IT UP. AND I ASK THAT YOU'LL USE ME (ESPECIALLY WITH ANNA PARKER). AND I PRAY THAT LOTS OF KIDS WILL GET SAVED BECAUSE I CAN SEE HOW MUCH THEY NEED YOU. THANKS SO MUCH FOR USING ME DESPITE ALL MY FLAWS! AMEN.

Saturday, January 26 (cool night)

We had another get-together at our church tonight. This time the church chipped in and ordered pizzas for the entire group. (Although Beanie talked Pizza Hut into a discount, it still had to cost a bundle!) Unfortunately, Beanie and Jenny both had to work tonight (making all those pizzas), but even without Beanie, Joel came anyway. And he acted as DJ, playing his CDs again, and mostly we just hung out and talked and ate and stuff.

Some kids danced (which was pretty funny when some of the old funky tunes were playing) and some

played games (Tony and Greg had rounded up a bunch
of games—everything from Twister to Monopoly). And it
was a pretty laid-back and mellow time, but good. I think
the group was only about half as big as last week's
crowd. Some of the rowdier kids didn't show up at all
(which I think was too bad in a way), but I suppose we're
just a little too tame for them. Also, we heard there was
a big drinking party happening on the other side of town,
which may have lured them away.

But the best part about tonight (for me) was when
Anna showed up. She came about midway through with
her friend Jewel Garcia. I don't know Jewel all that well,
but suffice it to say, she's a colorful character. And she
really likes the boys—and they like her. Anyway, I
headed straight their way, and thankfully there was
still some pizza and sodas left. Then we kind of stood
around and talked for a while. Just when we ran out of
things to say, Jamal came over and talked us into joining
them for what turned out to be a pretty wild game of
UNO. And Anna won, which I think made her happy.

All in all, it was a fun night. And, no, I don't think anyone got saved. Greg certainly didn't perform an altar
call. But just the same, I feel pretty convinced that God
was at work. I thought about the times Jesus spent with
people, eating and talking and having fun. Did you know
that some people (I think some of the overly religious
types) actually called Jesus a glutton and a drunkard?
All because he hung out with ordinary people and just
basically enjoyed their company while they shared food

and drink. Josh shared this little tidbit with me in his e-mail this week. It was a good reminder to me tonight (when I started feeling like I needed to "save" someone) that it's okay just to hang out and have fun. And I think Anna might even trust me more now. And, no, she didn't say she'd come to church with me tomorrow. But that's okay. Maybe next week. I think to start off with I need to show her that I'm willing to be her friend whether she comes to church with me or not. So I've decided to invite her to go do something else. I'm still not exactly sure what, but I think God will show me.

DEAR GOD, THANKS FOR WHAT YOU'RE TEACHING ME ABOUT REACHING OUT TO OTHERS. I ADMIT THAT I SOMETIMES THINK I HAVE TO DO SOME-THING SPECIAL TO HELP PEOPLE GET "SAVED." BUT I THINK THE TRUTH IS: <u>ONLY YOU CAN DO THAT</u>. PLEASE HELP ME TO RELY ON YOU MORE AND MORE AND MORE! AND PLEASE SHOW ME WHAT I CAN DO WITH ANNA TO HELP STRENGTHEN OUR FRIEND-SHIP. I'M AFRAID SHE STILL ISN'T TOO SURE WHAT TO MAKE OF ME, BUT I REALLY DO LIKE HER FOR WHO SHE IS—EVEN IF SHE'S NOT WALKING WITH YOU RIGHT NOW. AND YET I KNOW SHE NEEDS YOU, LORD. I CAN SEE IT IN HER EYES. AMEN.

FIVE

Thursday, January 31 (true confessions)

I am so thankful to have a diary to pour out my troubles to. And right now I'm about to make a confession that I'm not very proud of—in fact, it's pretty embarrassing. The thing is: I am jealous—yep, absolutely lime green with envy. For months I've acted like everything's just peachy-keen, and sometimes I've even believed my own little act myself. But the ugly truth is: I am just plain jealous of Beanie and Jenny's friendship. Ever since they started living together at my grandma's house, they've gotten closer and closer. And now with this whole dating dilemma tacked on—well, I basically feel left out. And I know that sounds totally lame (like a second grader whining "You like Jenny more'n you like me.") And it basically just makes me sick. Of course there's no way on God's green earth that I can tell those two what's bugging me. I mean, sheesh, I'd sound like an absolute idiot. I've already put myself at odds with them over enough other stupid things. Besides that, I was the one who tried so hard to get them to become friends in the first place—but talk about two completely different people. Who ever would've thought they'd get this close? But they are. And it's bugging the snot out of me.

I mean, like today for instance. I asked them if they wanted me to give them a ride to the basketball game tomorrow night. (Since it's an away game and neither of them have a car and I know they don't have to work.) But then Jenny says that Trent is taking them, and then Joel is going to join them afterward and they're all going out for a late dinner. Well, I acted all cool and stuff, saying "great, that's fine" and pretending like I could care less. But I was steamed. Really steamed. And it makes me feel like a pretty hopeless Christian too. Although I'm starting to realize that God doesn't really expect me to be perfect but just to try my best and stay connected to Him. And I'm trying. But I can see I still have a long, long ways to go.

So there you have it—Caitlin O'Conner is jealous—nah-nah-nah. Sigh... I think I feel a little bit better now. Sometimes you just need to get these things out. Even if it's only in a diary. Of course, the next step would be to pray about it.

DEAR GOD, I KNOW IT'S TOTALLY STUPID TO FEEL LIKE THIS, BUT I'M SURE YOU UNDERSTAND. AND IT'S NOT LIKE I WANT BEANIE AND JENNY TO SUD-DENLY HATE EACH OTHER. BUT I DO FEEL BAD. I

FEEL LEFT OUT. PLEASE SHOW ME HOW I CAN DEAL WITH THIS. AMEN.

Friday, February 1 (big aha!)

Well, today I was trying real hard not to be jealous (or at least not to show it). And we were having lunch just like normal when I noticed Anna Parker coming in late, and she was looking for a place to sit down. So I skooched over close to Beanie and waved, inviting Anna to join us (which is no big deal; we've all been sitting together lately anyway). But as soon as she sat down, I got the bright idea (actually I think it was God inspired) to ask her if she wanted a ride to the game tonight, and she said, "Sure."

So I told her I'd pick her up after work (well, after I zipped home to change, that is). Then she asked where I worked and I told her about how I'd gotten a reception job at my dad's office. She thought that was pretty cool and said she'd been trying to get an office job for after school too, and she'd already taken all the business classes available. Suddenly I remembered that I'd noticed another part-time receptionist position posted on the bulletin board in the break room. I'd even toyed with applying for it myself but had felt just a little intimidated since it was an "executive" position. Plus I really like working with Rita and was afraid it would hurt her feelings if I tried to switch jobs. (Besides, what if I didn't get the position?) So as a result I decided to do nothing at all.

"You know, there's an opening where I work, Anna," I

began. "I think it's still available. Just part time—the same hours as I'm working. The receptionist wants to be able to leave earlier so she can go home and spend more time with her kids.

"You're kidding!" Anna stared at me like I'd just offered her a million bucks. "That sounds perfect!"

Beanie poked me with her elbow. "Hey, how come you didn't tell me about that job?"

"You already have a job, Beanie."

"Yeah, but not a good job like that."

I rolled my eyes at her. "Well, you never mentioned wanting to switch jobs. And I thought it worked out pretty nice for you and Jenny to work at the same place. Besides—" I turned back to Anna again—"Anna's already taken the right kind of classes."

Anna was beaming now. And I must admit I felt a tiny twinge of satisfaction when I tossed out that part about Beanie and Jenny working in the same place. (Okay, God, forgive me!)

"Caitlin," said Anna, "do you really think I'd have a chance?"

"I don't know why not." Then I asked her when her last class was, and it turned out to be fifth period (same as me), so I invited her to ride over to work with me and check it out. Lucky for Anna, she always dresses pretty nice for school. Okay, it's a little too preppy and conservative for my taste, and I guess some kids probably think she's kind of old-fashioned, but I think it looks pretty good on her and it was perfect for going in for a job.

When we got to the office I introduced her to Rita, then gave her a quick tour, and finally took her up to personnel, where it turns out she not only filled out her application but also managed to land an interview. Pretty cool. Then she decided to hang around in the lobby (doing her homework) until I got done and could give her a ride home. When we got to her neighborhood, which is a little rundown, she asked me to drop her off in front of the apartments, saying she'd just run up and change for the game, if I didn't mind waiting down here. I told her that was fine. But I suspect she didn't want me to see where she lived. The reason I think this is because of my friendship with Beanie over the years. It was a long time before Beanie ever let me see the inside of her house. But I didn't know how to tell Anna I was used to this kind of thing, so I just kept my mouth shut.

As I sat there, I really prayed for her. And I prayed for our friendship because it suddenly feels like this is meant to be. I mean, maybe this is why I'm feeling so left out with Jenny and Beanie lately. So, who knows, maybe this is what God was up to all along.

Anyway, we ran by my house real quick, and I invited Anna up to my room while I quickly changed into jeans, then we nuked a couple of burritos in the microwave and snagged some sodas from the fridge and basically split. Oh, yeah, I did introduce her to my mom and Ben before we dashed out the door.

"You guys look like the all-American family," Anna said as we drove to the game.

I groaned. "That sounds pretty dull. But I suppose you're right. Although we were almost the all-American split-up family just a year ago." Then I told her a little about my dad's "almost" affair (I didn't think he'd mind under the circumstances) because I wanted Anna to know we're not perfect. Although I have to admit my family (despite their flaws) are pretty cool. And I like that we all go to church together, although Ben's been complaining about it a little lately (which has me concerned).

"My parents got divorced when I was a baby," Anna explained. "I have an older brother, but he's been gone for a while now. So it's just me and my mom."

I nodded. "That's how it was with Beanie. I mean, just her and her mom. But she doesn't live at home anymore." Then I told her a little about Lynn Jacobs (feeling fairly certain that Beanie wouldn't mind since she's pretty up-front about her family life these days). "But Lynn's doing a lot better now," I told her. "She's quit drinking, and my aunt Steph helped her get a good job where she works. Beanie says she may even move back home after my grandma gets back from Arizona."

"Sounds like things are going well for everyone." Anna took a swig of soda then sighed. "I guess it's that whole church thing—like you're all in one big, happy family. I guess I kind of envy that."

"Yeah, going to church doesn't hurt anything. But believe me it's not the fix-all for everything either. I mean, despite church, we've all had our problems—and then some. To be perfectly honest, I think we'd all be in a great big mess if it wasn't for God." Then I stopped myself. "But Anna, I really don't want to preach at you, and the truth is Beanie and Jenny sometimes accuse me of getting all preachy. And I'm really trying to break that habit."

Anna laughed. "It's okay. I probably need to hear a sermon or two."

I decided to change the subject anyway. "But it's funny that you should mention being jealous because I've really been struggling with that lately."

"You?" I could hear the skepticism in her voice.

I nodded. "Yep. I hadn't really planned on telling this to anyone. I mean, it's kind of embarrassing. But you see Beanie's been my best friend for years, and then I became friends with Jenny. And now the two of them are such good friends that I'm feeling pretty left out." I forced a laugh. "Pretty juvenile, huh?"

"So, is that why you invited me to come with you tonight?" Again I could hear a trace of something slightly skeptical or suspicious.

I shrugged. "Well, maybe to start with. I mean, I probably never would've thought of inviting anybody to come with me if Beanie and Jenny hadn't left me out in the cold. To be honest, I've never really been that outgoing with new friends. Although that's been changing lately."

Anna nodded. "Yeah, I've known you for a long time, and you always seem kind of quiet and shy. But you've always been nice to me."

I smiled. "Well, I think it's cool I'm getting a chance to

know you now. And if it wasn't for Beanie and Jenny being all buddy-buddy, it might not have happened. And I really hope you get that job too. Hey, you never told me how the interview went."

Anna didn't seem too sure. And I could tell that she doesn't have the most self-confidence, but then I can relate because I don't usually either.

Anyway, we had a good time at the game and stopped and got burgers afterward. And I asked her what her friend Jewel was doing tonight.

"You probably haven't heard, but Jewel has managed to snatch Jamal from Natala," Anna told me in a conspiratorial tone.

"You're kidding. I'll bet Natala is furious. I mean, she's pretty territorial, isn't she?"

Anna nodded. "Yeah, she's threatening to beat Jewel up. You know Natala hates Hispanics almost as much as whites."

I made a face. "Poor Jewel. She'd better watch her backside."

"I warned Jewel it was a totally stupid move. But she just wouldn't listen."

"Yeah, I'm finding it doesn't really do much good to tell your friends what to do." I laughed. "So, I should probably warn you that I've been accused of getting too involved with my friends' lives."

Anna smiled. "That's okay. I'm not worried."

And so I'm thinking this could be the beginning of a good friendship. And I'm really praying that Anna gets the job. I told her if she does, she can ride with me if she wants, and she seemed pretty hopeful. And I've decided to put in a good word for her with my dad. He's not at the top of the food chain there, but he does have a little clout and might be able to pull a few strings. But better than that, I can ask God—I know He can do anything!

PLEASE, GOD, I KNOW I ASK YOU FOR AN AWFUL LOT OF THINGS, BUT THIS TIME IT'S NOT EVEN FOR ME. SO, I'M JUST BEGGING YOU, PLEASE, PLEASE, PLEASE GIVE ANNA THAT RECEPTION JOB. THANK YOU (IN ADVANCE). AMEN.

Monday, February 4 (yippee!)

Well, I did put in a good word about Anna with my dad (as well as my heavenly Father). And she called from school this afternoon to find out she'd been scheduled for another interview. (She'd made the first cut!) So once again, she rode over to work with me, and I could tell she was getting real hopeful. But she also seemed really nervous.

"Do you think I look okay?"

"Yeah, Anna." I glanced over at her. "You look way better than me. I mean, you always look pretty professional, like you should be working in some big, fancy office building downtown."

She laughed nervously. "Yeah, Jewel always gives me a bad time about the way I dress. She thinks it's way

too conservative. But it's what I feel comfortable in. I figure people can take it or leave it."

I smiled. "It reminds me of Beanie. But she went the
opposite direction. She liked to dress kind of crazy-like,
just to see what people would do. But she got most of her
clothes secondhand, and so I suppose she was just making
the best of it."

Anna smoothed her hand over her navy wool skirt. "I
shop at thrift shops too."

"Wow, you'd never guess. I mean, you always look really
nice. I wasn't trying to say that was a bad thing—"

"It's okay, Caitlin. I know what you mean. But Jewel
makes fun of me sometimes, so I figured I'd just get it out
of the way."

I laughed. "I think it's cool you can find such good
stuff secondhand." Then I got an idea for the Mexico
kids, but we were already at work and I decided to
keep it until later.

But here's the really great news—Anna got the
job! Oh, man, was she ever happy. She stayed around
until I got off again, and then we went for coffee to
celebrate. And honestly, she seemed almost like a
different girl. Her face was just glowing with excitement.

"Caitlin, I can't believe it," she said. "I really didn't
think I had a chance. And I'm so grateful to you—for
everything. This is so great!"

With our coffee mugs we said a toast to our new
friendship and a long working relationship. And then Anna

smiled and said she'd like to come to church with me next Sunday!

Wednesday, February 6 (concerns)

I'm a little worried about Mom today. She hasn't been feeling very well this week (or maybe even longer although she hadn't said anything), and today she actually missed work and went to the doctor (and I can't ever remember her doing anything like that before). When she came home from the doctor, she just went to bed without saying anything.

I tried to make myself helpful by fixing dinner, but it seemed weird not having Mom around. Dad said not to worry, that she'd probably just been working too hard, but then he turned in early too. And I could hear their voices talking steadily and quietly and something about it all seemed serious. But maybe I'm just imagining things. I hope so.

Rita (at work) was telling me how her sister had been recently diagnosed with breast cancer and was scheduled for surgery today—and I promised to pray for her (which I've been doing). But suddenly I'm thinking, what if something like that happened to Mom? What would I do? And suddenly I'm realizing just how much I love her. I'd like to go in and tell her, but then that's probably dumb. And it might worry her more. Besides, I'm sure nothing is wrong. She's probably just tired. Just the same, I'll be helping out a lot more around the house.

And I'll get on Ben's case too. He could be a little more helpful.

> DEAR GOD, I'M SURE MY MOM IS FINE. BUT JUST IN CASE, I'M ASKING YOU TO WATCH OVER HER. JUST THINKING HOW SHE COULD BE SICK MAKES ME REALIZE HOW MUCH I LOVE HER AND HOW MUCH I NEED HER. SO IF SHE IS SICK, LORD, I ASK THAT YOU'LL PLEASE MAKE HER WELL. THANK YOU. AMEN.

SIX

Thursday, February 7 (strange stuff...)

Now this just totally takes the cake!
Tonight at dinnertime, Mom says she has an announcement to make, and I'm freaking, thinking she's going to tell
us she has cancer or something. But no, that's not it.
Instead she sits there and calmly tells us she's going to
have a baby—my mom is pregnant! Now, I'm sitting there
thinking this is pretty absurd. I mean, my mom isn't
ancient or anything, and I'll admit she looks pretty good
for her age, but good grief, the woman is forty-two years
old. Of course I don't want to say this, and to my utter
amazement she is smiling and seems almost happy about
the whole thing. But I do ask one little question.

"Uh, aren't you a little old to be having a baby?"

Well, I can tell by the look on her face that that's not
the right thing to say. But first she forces a little laugh.
Then she gets more serious. "Caitlin, I know this must seem
really strange to you kids." Ben's just sitting there wide-

eyed saying nothing, but he looks like someone swiped his Game Boy or something. Then Mom continues, "But you know a lot of women my age are having babies nowadays. It's not that unusual."

I nod as if I understand, but the truth is, I don't! I mean, I don't get it at all. Did they plan this thing? And if so, what were they thinking? But even my dad seems kind of stunned. (Although I suspect he's already heard the news by now.) So I decide I better just play it cool, and I paste a little smile onto my face and say, "Hey, that's great, Mom. It'll be fun having a little brother or sister. When is the baby due?"

"I'm not completely sure, but probably late summer."

"So will you go back to work in the fall then?"

Mom glances at Dad with some uncertainty. "We haven't figured all that out yet. Everything's still so new."

I nod again, trying to act like this is all just the greatest news when I'm really thinking, Hey, what about me? I mean, just when I've decided to go to college for sure, my mom gets herself pregnant. And I'm thinking how there's this big billboard by our high school saying how much it costs to have and raise a baby—and let me tell you, it's pretty scary! And I happen to know that my college savings aren't very big. (Dad explained this to me recently when he suggested I apply for any scholarships available.)

So now I'm feeling a little bit like that old boat that's been cut loose and is drifting out to sea—like bon voyage, baby, and have a good trip. Okay, okay, I know that's probably an overreaction on my part. But, sheesh, this feels kind of tough. I think about calling Beanie, but then I'm not totally sure how she'd react, and I wouldn't be all that surprised if she was in my mom's court on this. (I mean, it wasn't all that long ago that Beanie was wanting to be a mommy too—in fact, her baby probably would've been being born around now.) So I decide that's not a good idea. And I can't call over there and only talk to Jenny.... I consider Anna, but we're not quite that close yet. And so I decide to call Aunt Steph. She's usually pretty dependable with stuff like this. But guess what? I no sooner spring the news on Steph when she's beside herself with laughter. Now I'm thinking, I really don't see the humor in this. And when she finally gets control, she says, "I gotta go, Catie, but I'll be right over." So now I'm thinking, great—I wonder what I've started here. I'm not even sure my mom wanted anyone else to know about this, and here I've gone and spilled the beans.

So Steph comes over and grabs my mom and starts gushing. And as it turns out, Steph thinks she may be pregnant too! Oh, man, this is just too much for me. So I kind of smile and nod and wish them both well, then go slinking up to my room (saying I've got homework). So there you have it: Mom and Steph are going to be pregnant together. I suppose it's kind of cute in a weird way. And I think it's cool that Oliver will have a younger sibling. In fact, I suppose it might even be fun having a couple of little babies around to snuggle with. Especially since I'll (hopefully) be off to college about the time they're desperately looking for baby-sitters. Poor Ben!

DEAR GOD, PLEASE FORGIVE ME FOR MY BAD ATTI-
TUDE. OBVIOUSLY IF YOU WANT TO BRING TWO NEW
BABIES INTO OUR FAMILY, IT'S A GREAT THING. I
PRAY THAT YOU KEEP MOM AND STEPH IN YOUR
CARE. AND ONCE AGAIN, I'M SORRY ABOUT REACT-
ING SO NEGATIVELY. I'LL TRY TO DO BETTER.
AMEN.

Saturday, February 9 (seeds planted?)

We had another get-together at the church tonight.
Everything was pretty much like before, but Greg sort of
took the lead this time (since Joel seemed to be feeling
down—maybe because they lost their game last night).
But as a result it seemed like things got a little more
serious, which I think was probably good. Unfortunately
Beanie and Jenny both had to work tonight, so they
missed out. But after Greg explained how life gets lonely
sometimes and how we all need a friend like Jesus in our
lives, he invited anyone who wanted to know more about
it to talk to him privately. And I noticed that he and Joel
slipped away for a little while. Now I'm wondering if Joel
might've actually made a commitment. But I didn't want
to act like a snoop and ask him, and I sure couldn't ask
Greg. (I think that's privileged information.) So, I'll just
have to wait and see if Beanie mentions it. In the meantime, I'll be praying for Joel.

Anna came too (I picked her up). And tomorrow I'll pick
her up for church too. I'd be glad to pick up Jenny and
Beanie too, but they haven't asked me yet. And so I

decided to wait and see if they call. It's not like I'm trying to be mean or anything, but I'm thinking I've been
pretty pushy with them lately, and maybe I just need to
back off and chill a little.

Anna and I hung out together and it was cool. I think
our friendship is starting to really gel. And I'm finding out
she's pretty interesting too. In fact, we have a lot in common. We've read and really like the same books. And she
keeps a journal too. She's worked on the school paper and
yearbook and thinks she wants to major in journalism in
college, although she's worried about tuition since her
mom can't afford to help her. I told her she wasn't the
only one worried. Then under the cloak of confidence, I
explained about my mom's little surprise, but I asked Anna
not to tell anyone since both Mom and Steph are keeping
their news quiet for a while. Actually, Steph admitted
she hasn't even done a pregnancy test yet but has a
strong feeling. But Anna said I can trust her and that
she's used to keeping secrets. I wasn't sure what she
meant by that. But anyway, she starts work on Monday
and is so excited you'd think she'd won the lottery.

DEAR GOD, PLEASE KEEP DOING WHATEVER IT IS
YOU'RE DOING TO GET THESE KIDS INTERESTED
IN KNOWING YOU. I PRAY FOR JOEL, IF HE MADE A
COMMITMENT (OR EVEN IF HE DIDN'T), THAT YOU'D
JUST MAKE HIM WANT YOU MORE THAN ANYTHING
ELSE. AND I PRAY FOR ANNA TOO. PLEASE HELP HER
TO SEE YOU WANT TO BE HER FRIEND. I CAN SEE

SHE'S HURTING INSIDE, EVEN IF SHE PUTS ON A
BRAVE FACE. PLEASE SHOW HER HOW MUCH YOU
LOVE HER. AMEN.

Sunday, February 10 (great day!)

After youth group, Anna went back to talk to Greg. Then
later after church, she told me that she'd invited Christ
back into her heart. I could tell she'd been crying. We
just hugged, and I told her how glad I was and that I'd
been praying for her. Joel was sitting with Beanie and
Jenny, and I had a feeling he's made the same commitment too. I can't wait to find out for sure. But they all
had to leave right after youth group because Beanie
and Jenny both had to work again today. Sometimes I
feel sorry for those two. It seems they have to work all
the time and miss out on a lot of fun stuff. Like after
church today when Anna and I went over to the mall
and just hung out and relaxed for a while.

"I think we're lucky," I told Anna as we ate cinnamon
rolls at the food court (my treat to celebrate her recom-
mitment to Jesus). "Only having to work after school during the weekdays sounds lots better than what Beanie
and Jenny have to put up with."

She nodded. "Yeah, but I may have to get a job during the weekends too."

"Why's that?"

"I need to start getting more serious about saving for
college. Right now I have only enough for maybe one
semester."

"Oh. Yeah, I guess I should think about that too."
Then I frowned.

"What's wrong?"

"I guess I feel kind of torn." I thought for a moment, then decided to go ahead. I explained to her about the mission trip our youth group had taken to Mexico last summer and about the deprived children we discovered at the garbage dump and how I wanted to help. "So, you see, I've been trying to send money and stuff. But now I'm wondering if I should cut back. But then I hate to do that."

"That is so cool, Caitlin."

"Huh?"

"I mean, that you care so much about those kids. That's totally cool."

I smiled. "Well, if you'd been there and seen them, I'm sure you'd have felt the same way. It was pretty sad. But that reminds me of something. I was thinking about how you're so good at finding nice things at thrift shops and stuff. And I thought maybe you'd like to help me. I try to get used kids' clothes to send, and maybe the thrift shops would like to help donate—you know, things that might not sell that well here but would be great for down there where they have practically nothing. Some of the kids only had filthy underwear to wear."

She nodded. "Sure, I'd be glad to ask around. I've gotten to know a couple of shops pretty well." She glanced uncomfortably around the mall. "In fact, I usually make it a habit to avoid places like this."

"Why's that?"

She frowned. "Well, it's kind of like being the kid standing outside of the candy store, if you know what I mean."

"Yeah, I know what you mean. And if it makes you feel any better, I don't usually buy much here anymore. I just look around and hang with my friends. Oh, I might get something small and inexpensive. But I don't spend money here like I used to. Since going to Mexico I've started thinking differently about some things. It's kind of embarrassing sometimes though."

"Why?"

"Well, some of my friends—not Beanie, of course—but like Jenny and Andrea, well, they're kind of used to being pretty free and easy with their spending. Anyway, Jenny used to be. She's had to tighten up since she's not living at home anymore. But Beanie told me that Jenny's dad has been giving her money from time to time, so she's not exactly penniless either. Not like Beanie's been."

"Or like me."

"Well, that's going to change soon." I grinned. "I know the pay's not the greatest there, but it sure beats the fast-food places."

Then we just walked around and looked at stuff for a while. I took Anna to a really expensive store, explaining how Beanie and I would "just look" in there sometimes, and then Beanie would get ideas for ways she could find similar pieces of used clothing and adapt them to look like a designer original—or even better. "Although she could come up with some pretty strange looking outfits too." I laughed. "But then it's her own personal style."

Anna looked at a shirt I was checking out, then frowned. "I'm just no good at fashion. Sometimes I wish I were, because I know I probably look like a nerd most of the time—at least that's what Jewel always says. But then she dresses so flashy that I think she looks like a hooker half the time, so I sure don't go asking her for fashion advice." Then Anna turned and stared at me. "But you always look nice, Caitlin. I like your style."

I smiled. "Gee, thanks, I didn't realize I actually had a style." Then I held the shirt up in front of her and made her look in the mirror. "Hey, that looks pretty cool on you."

She studied it. "I guess so."

I sneaked a peek at the price tag then gulped. "One hundred and eighty-five dollars," I said under my breath.

"You're kidding!"

I grinned and shook my head, then gingerly replaced the shirt back on the rack as if it were made of fine gold.

"I bet I could find something almost like it at the thrift shop."

"Why don't you?"

"Well, I just might."

She continued studying her image in the mirror. "But

even so, I think there's something about me that doesn't quite work."

I looked at her, suddenly feeling uncertain. I mean, Anna and I may have a lot in common, but our appearance is pretty different. Besides, who was I to advise her on style? Then again, isn't that what friends are for? Beanie and Jenny and I never worry about hurting each other's feelings when it comes to fashion. "Well, have you ever considered wearing your hair differently?"

She reached up and ran her hand over her tightly pulled back hair. Ever since I can remember, Anna's always worn her hair combed flat and pulled back into a small ponytail that looks more like a bun. She usually has a barrette or a scrunchie wrapped around it, but it's always the exact same look. And in my opinion, it only serves to make her face look broader. But I wasn't going to say that.

Suddenly I noticed a sales clerk eyeing us, and I knew it was time to move on. "Maybe we should go," I whispered, glancing over my shoulder.

"Yeah, they probably think we've shoplifting." And the way she said it I could tell she was serious.

"I know, Anna, why don't you come over to my house and we'll see what we can do to change your look—I mean, if you want to, that is." Now I wondered if I'd gone too far. I sure didn't want to hurt her feelings. And I knew our friendship wasn't all that stable yet.

But she just smiled. "Sure, that sounds like fun. If you really want to. I mean, you don't have to—"

"Hey, there's not much else to do on a rainy Sunday afternoon. Why not go home and play dress up?"

Anna giggled as we ran through the rain to the car, and I'm sure it's the first time I'd heard her do so because usually she's so serious. "Yeah," she said, "I suppose it makes sense to do something with my outside appearance now since I've already done something with my inside."

"Yeah, I wanted to ask you how that all went, but I hate to be all nosy and everything."

"Oh, it's okay to ask. In fact, I'm feeling really great on the inside. I prayed before I went to bed last night. And I prayed again this morning. And it's amazing—there was all this stuff I was worried about, and I don't feel quite so bad now. I guess I really needed Jesus more than I knew. I can see now how I was carrying a bunch of things on my own—like what am I supposed to do with my life, or why I am the way I am.... I know it sounds kind of silly, but I think it was sucking the life out of me."

"No, it doesn't sound silly at all." I assured her. "I know just what you mean." Then I told her a little bit about me when I first got saved and how I had all these questions and doubts and fears... And it was cool; she really seemed to relate and understand.

Anna and I spent the rest of the afternoon in my room and had the best time giving her a complete makeover. I even dug out Mom's old Mary Kay kit and we experimented with some makeup samples that looked pretty cool on her. And when my aunt Steph just happened to drop by, I enticed her (with the promise of free baby-sitting) to cut Anna's hair (naturally Anna had agreed first), and Aunt Steph (who could've been a beautician if she wanted) gave Anna this great-looking cut with layers and soft bangs and Anna looked absolutely fantastic. Aunt Steph has naturally curly hair too and understands how it needs to be cut and conditioned to lie just right. So she explained all this to Anna, and it really seemed to work too. Then I had Anna try on some of my clothes, and we discovered that we wear almost exactly the same size, which is kind of fun since Beanie is bigger than me and Jenny is smaller. Finally, I asked Anna if she really liked her glasses. They're not too terrible really (just plain tortoiseshell rims, but a little on the chunky side). Then she told me she has contacts but never wears them.

"I feel kind of bad too because I know my mom paid a lot of money for them when she really couldn't afford to. But at the time it kind of made me mad, because I hadn't even asked for them and she acted like it was some big sacrifice and everything. I guess I just wanted to be stubborn."

I laughed. "Yeah, I know what you mean. Sometimes you just want your parents to know that it's your life and too much interference is not appreciated." Then I asked her to take off her glasses, and it was just like one of those old movies (that my grandma collects) where the secretary takes off her clunky glasses and looks just like a movie star.

"Anna!" I exclaimed. "Can you see yourself?"

She squinted. "Well, not really. I am nearsighted, you know."

I pushed her close to the mirror, but she still didn't seem to get it. So I snagged my purse and said, "We're going over to your place to get your contacts."

She laughed and grabbed her glasses and we were off.

To make a long story short, I waited in the car while she went up and put in her contacts. Then I drove her over to Pizza Hut for Jenny and Beanie to see. They just gushed over Anna until I'm afraid she was getting embarrassed, and finally we left and I drove her back home.

"Thanks, Caitlin," she said when I dropped her off. "For everything."

"I should be thanking you," I said honestly. "This was really fun."

And so there you have it: Anna Parker new on the inside and outside too. I hope that's okay. I hope I wasn't being too pushy. But she seemed to like it. Still, it occurs to me, now that it's all over and done, that she might perceive what we did as me wanting to change her. And I didn't. I think she was just fine the way she was. She's the one who seemed unhappy with her looks. I hope I didn't blow it.

DEAR GOD, PLEASE WATCH OVER ANNA AND KEEP HER HEART TUNED IN TO YOU. AND IF I WENT TOO

FAR WITH THAT MAKEOVER STUFF, I'M REALLY
SORRY. I KNOW I HAVE A TENDENCY TO BE PRETTY
SHALLOW SOMETIMES. BUT I DON'T MEAN ANY
HARM. PLEASE HELP OUR FRIENDSHIP TO GROW AND
STRENGTHEN. AMEN.

SEVEN

Tuesday, February 12 (truth or consequences)

I should know better than to check e-mail during my break at work. Not that it's not allowed, because you can do pretty much whatever you want on your break. Most of the time I don't even take a break, but occasionally I do check my e-mail, which is no big deal because it's not like I have a bunch of people writing to me. Mostly it's just junk mail (like ridiculous ads for some new miracle weight-loss ointment) that needs to be tossed. But today when I checked I had an e-mail from Josh—which is always a pleasant surprise. But not today.

I know I shouldn't care, I shouldn't react, I should be way above how I'm feeling right now, but the truth is I'm not. And here's another reason to be thankful for this diary—once again I can say how I really feel, even if I do sound totally confused and stupid. Aren't diaries great? Okay, the thing is: I just don't get why Josh wants to go to the Valentine's Day ball with some girl he barely even knows. Or why he felt the need to write and tell me all about it. As if he knows he's going to get some kind of reaction from me. Oh sure, he tells me, it's just the college pastor's kid sister who really wants to go to this dance but doesn't have a boyfriend to take her...yada, yada, yada—blah, blah, blah... I'm surprised he didn't say she was cross-eyed and had a face like a horse. Not that it should matter one way or another because it's really none of my business. Right?

Why on earth should I even care? Furthermore, what am I supposed to say to him in response? Maybe the part that bugs me the most about this whole thing is how I could tell (at least I think I could) that Josh was already questioning himself in this decision. I mean, wasn't it just last fall when he said that (like me) he'd given up on dating altogether? But now this. Of course, he said that this wouldn't be an "official date," whatever that means. So if it's not a date, then what is it? But if he sounds like he's compromising his convictions, and he's writing all about it to me, does that mean that I should set him straight? Ha-ha-ha! Just who am I to set anyone straight on anything? (Ask Jenny and Beanie!) And even if I were to write back and tell him I was a little concerned about his choice here, who's to say how pure my motives might be in this whole thing?

Because, if the truth were told—and I'm not entirely sure I could actually tell it to myself or anyone else (but hopefully God knows)—I might actually be in love with Josh Miller. Yikes, I can't even believe I really wrote that! What if I were to say that he shouldn't date anyone ever—just to preserve my chances with him? (How's that for a healthy confession?) Now, I'm not saying I really _am_ in love with Josh or that I _know_ he's absolutely the one God wants me to marry someday. But I'm not saying he's not either. Still, what if my response to him ended up being some desperately lame attempt to keep my options with him open? Pretty pitiful, isn't it? And totally ridiculous too. Okay, just slap me, somebody!

Anyway, that's the reason I still haven't replied to his e-mail. I wanted to pour out my feelings into my diary first, hoping I'd get some clarity here or at least recognize how selfish and foolish I sound (which I can easily see now). But at the same time, I'm feeling more confused than ever. Not so much about Josh as about myself.

I do know this one thing for sure though: I do love Josh. Now I may not actually be in love with him (although I'm not so sure I'm not either). But I do love him as a brother and as a dear friend. And I guess that means I really want whatever's best for him (even if it doesn't appear to be best for me). And I do know the very best thing for him (or anyone for that matter) is to take our really tough decisions to God and ask Him to lead and guide us. And so that's exactly what I'll write back to Josh. The funny thing is, it's just the kind of thing he would write to me. I guess sometimes we need to be reminded of what we already know. But isn't that what brothers and sisters are for?

DEAR GOD, I'M SO INCREDIBLY GLAD YOU ALREADY KNOW EVERYTHING THAT'S INSIDE OF ME (AND YOU LOVE ME ANYWAY!). YOU KNOW MY HEART AND WHAT MAKES ME TICK. YOU KNOW IF I'LL EVER MARRY AND WHO IT'LL BE IF I DO. I REALIZE NOW THAT I HAVE NO BUSINESS TRYING TO INFLUENCE JOSH ONE WAY OR ANOTHER ON THIS. ALL I CAN DO IS DIRECT HIM BACK TO YOU AND LET HIM KNOW I'M STILL HIS LOYAL FRIEND, NO MATTER WHAT. THANKS FOR SETTING ME STRAIGHT ON THIS, GOD. I NEEDED THAT! AMEN.

Wednesday, February 13 (confessions)

On the way home from work, I had to drive really carefully since it was starting to rain and sleet and cars were spinning out all over the place. So as I put-tered along, I mentioned Josh's e-mail to Anna. (I really hadn't meant to, but I suppose I was still slightly con-cerned that I hadn't heard back from him yet.) And bringing up Josh, of course, naturally led into my whole nondating thing (which I don't particularly enjoy shar-ing with others—just because it usually entails so much explaining, plus I've discovered lately how it can come across as judgmental or superior to some people). So I tried to tiptoe around the whole thing a little, hoping we'd quickly move on to something else. But as it turned out, Anna was really interested in the whole thing. And she was surprisingly understanding and really easy to talk to.

"Yeah, I've never really dated much," she admitted. "Mostly because I've been pretty shy. But to be honest, the few times I did go out—usually on a double date with Jewel and her boyfriend at the time—it would usually turn into a real disaster." She groaned as if remembering something particularly bad.

"Yeah, I know what you mean. It's like all the rules change when you're on a date. And suddenly there's all these expectations, and one thing leads to another, and before you know it you feel like you're in over your head—"

"And going down fast!" Anna added. Then we both laughed.

"I don't mind going out in groups so much," I told her, remembering the times when Beanie and Zach and Josh and I did things together. Sometimes it was kind of fun. "But then if some of the other couples get too serious, it can get a little uncomfortable."

"Tell me about it!" She shook her head. "Going out with Jewel and her various boyfriends was usually worse than being stuck in the front row of the movie theater during a really raunchy sex scene."

I had to laugh at that picture.

"But I think it could be different," she said wistfully. "I mean, I think I'd like to go out on a really good date sometime, with a guy who's not a setup, a guy who I really like. I think that could be fun."

I just shrugged. "Yeah, I suppose—maybe under the right conditions." Although I was really thinking maybe not.

Well, okay, maybe if I were older and seriously thinking about marriage—maybe then it'd be okay. I think I could imagine some kind of mature dating (like if I was engaged), and in a way it sounds like it could be fun going out with the man you love and plan to marry. But even so, we'd have to keep God in the center of our relationship.

So anyway, we'd reached her house by then and I waited as usual for her to reach into the back and grab her pack, but then she paused. "You know, Caitlin, I feel kind of bad that I've never asked you to come inside."

"Oh, that's okay—"

"No." She shook her head. "It's not okay. Because in the past couple days, I feel like God is showing me that I need to let go of some things—like my pride for one thing." She sighed. "You see, it's my pride that doesn't want you to see where I live—or meet my mom. And I know that's wrong."

I reached over and put my hand on her shoulder. "You know, Anna, if it makes you feel any better, Beanie and I have been really good friends for years. And it took her quite a while before she let me see where she lived. And it's pretty bad where she lived—most likely much worse than your home."

Her eyebrows shot up. "Really?"

"Yeah, I mean, I wouldn't usually tell anyone. But her place was usually pretty filthy, and Beanie's mom was almost always stoned or drunk. And then her boyfriends would come and go, and well, just take my word for it—it was bad."

Anna nodded. "I know homes that are like that—maybe worse."

"You won't repeat this to anyone, will you?"

She shook her head. "No way. But next time you come to pick me up, our apartment number is 14D. Just come on up and knock on the door—if you want to, that is."

I smiled. "Sure, I'd like to see where you live."

She kind of cringed.

"Really, Anna. You'd be surprised at how much I've hung out at Beanie's house over the years. I guess I'm a lot tougher than I look."

I waved and watched as she dashed toward her building, getting pelted by sleet that was falling even faster now. But what I said was the truth. After I'd gotten over my initial shock at Beanie's, I always found it kind of fascinating. It was like walking into a whole different world. Besides that, you never felt like you had to keep your feet off the furniture or be real careful not to spill things. (It was about the same time when my mom picked out this really light-colored carpet for our whole house, and she made us take off our shoes before walking on it. Plus you really have to watch things like grape juice or colored soda—thank goodness, she's mellowed out a little since then.) So being in a place that's more relaxed was always kind of fun—not to mention interesting. Anyway, I'm glad Anna feels comfortable enough to invite me over. And I think when I see where she lives, I'll probably even understand her better too.

Thursday, February 14 (Happy Valentine's Day to me!)

As I was getting ready for school this morning, I had on the Christian radio station as usual, and they were giving out free concert tickets to the seventh caller. So I decided to give it a try—and guess what? The next thing I know I'm on the air and the lucky winner of two Rachael Lampa concert tickets! I totally couldn't believe it. The concert's this Sunday night, and although I'd really wanted to go, I decided I couldn't spare the money (especially since I'm now trying to save for both college and the kids in Mexico). And anyway, it almost seemed like these tickets were like a special valentine from God. Yeah, I know that probably sounds silly, but since I'm out of the dating and romance scene, I like the idea of God giving me a valentine! I decided to invite Anna to join me (since she probably won't have any boys giving her a valentine today either).

I should've known that inviting Anna might make Beanie or Jenny jealous. But I couldn't take them both, and besides, they seem pretty happy in their own little world right now. And they've both got dates for the Valentine's dance tomorrow. I remember the dance last year (ugh!), and to be perfectly honest, I don't feel too bad about not going. Okay, maybe just a slight twinge of envy, but winning these concert tickets really helped take the edge off it. Anna is so excited and I promised to loan her my Rachael Lampa CD so she could get familiar with the songs. Rachael is about our age—maybe even younger. But she really sings for the Lord and she's totally amazing!

But after hearing the news, Beanie took me aside right after lunch. "What's up with you, Caitlin?" she asked in an irritated voice as we walked to our American lit class.

"Huh?"

"I mean, why are you acting so chilly to me lately?"

"What do you mean?"

"It's like we're hardly even friends anymore."

"Beanie," I began, "you'll always be my friend. You know that. But you've got to admit your life's been pretty full up lately."

She considered this. "Yeah, I suppose it seems that way."

"Seems that way?"

"Well, I know I've been pretty busy with work and Joel and Jenny and stuff. But I don't ever want to lose my friendship with you, Cate." And I'm pretty sure her eyes were getting misty just then. Maybe mine were too.

So right there in the Language Arts hallway, I hugged her. "Beanie, you know you'll never lose me. You've been the best friend I've ever had—and I really hope it always stays that way."

"Really?" She looked seriously surprised.

"Of course! I hope we're still friends when we're wrinkly, stooped-over, little, white-haired old ladies."

She laughed. And although it might not seem like such a big deal, it made me feel good inside that

Beanie still cared. I mean, I thought she probably did. But sometimes you just don't know for sure. Sometimes it's best to say these things out loud (even if you think the other person should know). And then we made a promise to do something special together soon—just the two of us.

"Just for the record, I do think it's cool how you and Anna have become so close. And I think Anna is really nice," she said quietly as we found seats. "But I guess I was a little jealous."

That's when Mr. Babcock started to lecture, or I'm sure I would've confessed to her all about my own recent and petty jealousies.

Saturday, February 16 (loose ends)

I finally got an e-mail from Josh. Yes, I know he's been busy with classes and whatever. And it's not like I just sit at my computer and wait for that little electronic voice to say "You've got mail!" Well, not exactly. But I guess I have checked it pretty regularly lately. Anyway, Josh thanked me for my response and told me that it sounded very mature and spiritual and that it helped him. Then he told me that he'd felt it was the right thing to take that girl (Anita) to the dance, but that he explained to her it wasn't like a romantic date or anything. And apparently she was perfectly fine with that. Then he reminded me of how it was okay for the apostle Peter to eat those foods. And how this was a little like that, and I suppose it all makes sense.

Anyway, I e-mailed back and told him that it sounded like he'd done the right thing, and perhaps, if a situation like that came up for me, I'd do the same thing too. Now, to be perfectly honest, I might've just tossed in that last line to see if he had any reaction to it. But before I could stop myself, I'd already hit the send button. Oh, well. I'm sure God can help me sort it out later. I'd also told him about winning the concert tickets and my new friendship with Anna. So hopefully he won't think the whole e-mail was about this dating thing. Because quite frankly, I'd like to move on now!

Sunday, February 17 (long night)

I felt uncomfortable leaving for the concert this afternoon because my mom was feeling kind of bad and Dad's been out of town on business for a few days (until tomorrow) and Ben was at a friend's house. So I called Aunt Steph and told her about my concern, even worrying as I did that I was sounding all paranoid again.

"What do you mean by feeling bad, Cate?" she asked.

"Well, she's been in bed most of the day and she says she feels kind of crampy and achy."

Steph groaned.

"Does that sound serious?"

"Did you tell her you were calling me?"

"Yeah, but she told me not to. She keeps saying she'll be just fine and not to worry. But I do feel worried. Maybe I should just stay home with her."

"No, Cate, you go to that concert. I'll leave Oli with Tony and come over and visit with your mom for a while."
"Are you sure?"

"Absolutely. You and Anna go and have fun. And don't worry so much, honey, okay?"

So I went ahead and picked up Anna at five (the concert was in the city—about ninety minutes from here). And we got there just in time to grab a bite to eat, park, and get our seats—which were in the THIRD row! And it was a totally awesome concert. Anna even cried (actually I think I did too), and it was just the greatest. I'm sure we were both on a real high coming home, and as a result the trip flew by.

Well, it was after midnight by the time I got home, but Tony's car was parked out in front and the lights were still on in the house, and suddenly I just knew something was wrong. I ran into the house to find little Oliver asleep under a blanket on the couch and Tony and Ben in the kitchen making cocoa.

"What's going on?" I demanded when I saw Ben's red-rimmed eyes, like he'd been crying real hard. "Where's Mom?"

"Everything's okay," said Tony. "Sit down and I'll explain."

So I sat down with my stomach twisting and turning and my hands shaking because I just totally knew something was wrong with Mom and I should've stayed home with her. Tony placed a mug of cocoa in front of me and then told me that Steph had taken Mom to the emergency room a few hours ago, and that Mom had an ectopic pregnancy, which he explained was when the fertilized egg gets stuck outside the womb. I glanced over at Ben and he seemed to understand all this, and I felt thankful that Tony had been here to handle this.

"But is she okay?" I felt my eyes filling with tears now.

"They've already operated on her and she's in recovery now."

"Is the baby okay?"

He looked down at the table and shook his head. "There was no chance of saving the baby. It had probably died several days ago. She just didn't know it at the time."

"Poor Mom." The tears started sliding down my cheeks now as I remembered her excitement about having a baby. And then I remembered my rotten attitude (even if I did manage to keep it under cover), and the tears started coming faster. "But maybe she can get pregnant again."

Tony cleared his throat, then glanced at Ben. "Well, I was waiting to tell you both this at the same time. But there's another problem too."

"What?" I felt my throat choking up now.

"Well, when they opened her up they discovered the reason for the problem. It seems your mother had a tumor."

"What does that mean?" Ben's voiced cracked and his eyes were huge. "Is that cancer?"

Just hearing Ben say that word sent real shivers down my back. "Is it cancer, Tony?"

"They'll send a sample out for a biopsy, but Steph said the doctor felt pretty sure it was benign."

"What's benign?" demanded poor Ben.

"It means it's not cancer," I said quickly. "Right, Tony?"

He nodded. "But they can't say for sure, and she may still need some treatments. They'll want to check her thoroughly to make sure she's clean throughout."

"Poor Mom," said Ben.

I put my arm around his sagging shoulders, noticing suddenly how wide they were getting to be. "She's going to be okay, Ben," I assured my little brother. Then we all three sat around the kitchen table and prayed for her for a while. By the time I drank my cocoa, it was scummy on the top and barely warm.

Then Aunt Steph called, and I asked her if I should come over to the hospital, but she said that Mom was just sleeping soundly now and would probably rest better knowing we were all safe at home.

I don't know where the phone number for Dad is, but he'll be flying out early in the morning. I guess he'll just have to hear about all this when he gets here.

But now it's after two, and I'm exhausted and have decided to just pray for my mom until I fall asleep, then I'll go over first thing in the morning.

EIGHT

Monday, February 18 (hard stuff)

Today has been really weird. It's like I'm seeing everything through a different set of eyes or something. When I went to visit Mom this morning, I felt kind of off-balance, like maybe the earth had rocked off its axis or something. I mean, it was so strange to see Mom just lying in the bed, looking so helpless and fragile. I kept expecting her to pop up and ask me what I wanted for breakfast (which I forgot to eat by the way). Anyway, she had on one of those awful hospital gowns in the most noxious shade of blue, with an IV tube sticking out of her arm. And I've never been one to like hospitals in the first place, but it made me feel just horrible to see her like that. Fortunately, Ben handled the whole thing surprisingly well; he even cracked a couple of totally lame jokes that actually made her smile, but I could tell she was still in pain. I just wished Dad would hurry up and get home. I'd left him a BIG note on the kitchen table telling him to call and come right over ASAP.

It wasn't too long before Steph stopped by. She'd taken the morning off, and, after dropping Oliver at nursery school, came in to check on things. I was so relieved to see her, mostly because I didn't know exactly what to say to Mom. I mean, I didn't know if I should mention the baby, or if that would make her feel worse. In some ways it felt like déjà vu. (You know, where it seems like you've done this exact thing before.) And suddenly I remembered how helpless I'd felt when Beanie lost her baby. But then that was so totally different. Still I was feeling this familiar feeling of guilt, like maybe if I had wanted that baby more, then this whole thing wouldn't have happened. Now I know it sounds crazy and egocentric and just totally ridiculous, but that's honestly how I felt. And as a result, I was feeling even worse for Mom. It's like I was ready to do anything to turn back the clock and make this all work out right for her.

So I went down to the lobby and just sat there and prayed and prayed—asking God to heal her so that she could get pregnant again and have that baby that she'd been so excited about. I was really feeling hopeful about the whole thing too, thinking this could turn out to be a really miraculous thing. Then Steph came down and met me in the lobby.

"Did Tony tell you everything?" she asked, her eyes shadowed with concern.

"Uh, yeah, I think so." I tried to remember his exact words. "He said she had a tumor, but that it had been removed, and that it was probably benign, but they'd send it to be checked anyway. He sounded like everything would be okay. It will, won't it?"

"Yeah, sure. But it's a little more involved than that. Your mom had to have a complete hysterectomy. And I think she's still feeling pretty upset about it."

I nodded dumbly.

"You understand that that means she won't be able to have a baby, don't you?"

I nodded again, although I hadn't been completely sure.

"And even though she says things like she's really too old to be having a baby, I still think she's taking it a lot harder than she's letting on."

"That sounds pretty much like Mom."

"And it's hard for me to be that much comfort to her, because here I am pregnant, you know?"

"Yeah, I can understand."

"So you might need to be the strong one here, Cate."

I swallowed hard, holding back new tears. "Sure, I can try to do that." I was afraid to tell Steph how I'd just been praying for Mom to be completely healed— afraid that I'd burst into tears if I admitted how I'd just felt so certain that everything would be fine and Mom would have her baby by this time next year. And to be honest, I felt a little disappointed in God too.

So Steph took Ben back to school, assuring him that everything was going to be okay, and I stayed with Mom until Dad got there around two o'clock. And it sounds bizarre, but it feels like I aged several years during those few hours. It's not like Mom and I talked that much or anything, but just being there and trying to be helpful and encouraging to her—it's like we'd switched roles. It was so weird. And I thought maybe that's why Beanie seems older a lot of the time, since she and her mom had switched roles so much over the years. But still it was weird.

And I can't remember when I've been so glad to see Dad. It's like he just swooped right in and knew exactly what to do. Without even taking off his coat, he wrapped his arms around my mom and she just started to sob. (I'm pretty sure he was crying too.) And seeing them there together like that just seemed so right, and so I slipped out. I'll admit I felt a little displaced for a moment or two, but mostly I felt relieved, like a heavy stone had been lifted off my chest. Just the same, I had to stop in the bathroom and wipe the tears off my face again.

Amazingly, I went ahead and went to work, stopping by the school first so I could pick up Anna. When I didn't show up at school, apparently she'd been pretty worried that something was wrong and then called my house to find nobody home. And she seemed genuinely saddened and concerned when I told her what had happened to Mom. When I dropped Anna home, she promised to be praying for Mom and the rest of us. I appreciated that.

DEAR GOD, I ADMIT I WAS FEELING A LITTLE MAD AT YOU EARLIER TODAY. BUT THEN I HAD TO REALIZE

THAT IT'S NOT YOUR FAULT MOM LOST HER BABY
AND WON'T BE ABLE TO HAVE ANY MORE.
ALTHOUGH I WONDER WHY YOU DIDN'T HELP PRE-
VENT THIS WHOLE THING IN THE FIRST PLACE,
WHICH I KNOW IS RIDICULOUS BECAUSE HARD
STUFF LIKE THIS HAPPENS EVERY DAY. AND I HAVE
A FEELING YOU JUST WANT US TO TRUST YOU
MORE AND GROW STRONGER AS A RESULT. LIKE
THAT VERSE IN JAMES ABOUT BEING THANKFUL
WHEN WE HAVE TOUGH TIMES BECAUSE WE KNOW
THAT IT WILL STRENGTHEN OUR FAITH. SO, I'M
ASKING YOU TO MAKE ME STRONGER, LORD. I
NEED YOUR HELP NOW. AMEN.

Wednesday, February 20 (slowly mending)

Mom's doing better, but I think she's depressed. And she won't be able to return to work for a few weeks. As a result, Ben and I are trying to be really helpful around the house. But it's like somebody put a damper of sadness around the whole place, like we've all sort of tiptoeing around and acting all polite and nice and just plain different. I'm sure it'll all go back to normal in time, but it makes me realize how much better I like it the other way. My dad's been coming home earlier too (bringing work home with him). And somehow I think my parents have gotten closer because of all this. Yet at the same time, I'm feeling a little on the outside these days. And I think Ben is too. So I'm trying to be a better sister. I even invited him to Friday's basketball game and told him he can invite a couple of buddies if he wants. He seemed to think that was pretty cool, and it was nice to see him smile again. All things considered, he's a good little brother.

DEAR GOD, PLEASE HELP ME NOT TO BE SELF-CENTERED. HELP ME TO THINK OF OTHERS FIRST (LIKE BEN AND MOM AND DAD). HELP ME TO LEARN HOW TO BE A BETTER SERVANT. HELP US ALL TO GET THROUGH THIS TIME. IT'D SURE BE NICE TO LAUGH TOGETHER AGAIN. AMEN.

Thursday, February 21

Today when I dropped Anna home from work, she invited me to come up and see where she lives. "Are you sure?" I asked thinking maybe it'd be better if I just got home so I could help get dinner started.

Her eyes brightened. "Yes, I think I can handle it now. If you have time, that is."

"Sure," I said, thinking maybe this was more important than I realized. "But maybe I should call Ben and tell him I'll be a few minutes late."

So I followed her up the narrow stairway bracing myself for a situation similar to Beanie's old home but then felt surprised and initially dismayed when Anna unlocked and opened the door to a fairly normal look-ing apartment. Sure, it was small and cramped, but it was all very neat and clean. In fact, with all the doilies and crocheted afghans on the chairs and sofa, it reminded me of when I was a little girl and visited my great-grandma's house before she passed away.

"This is nice," I told Anna as I glanced around. "Where's your mom?"

"She works late tonight."

I knew that her mom was a cook in a restaurant downtown and had slightly unpredictable hours.

"Do you want to sit down and have a soda?"

"Sure, let me call Ben first." I could tell by the way Anna was acting that having someone over was new to her, and she seemed pretty nervous. So I made my call and sat down before she came back with two glasses of Coke over ice.

"I don't see why you were so worried about this place." I waved my hand around. "It's really nice and neat and—" I ran out of words.

"And it looks like a little granny's house," she finished, eyeing me carefully.

"Well, I have to admit it reminded me of my great-grandma's place. But there's nothing wrong with that."

She rolled her eyes. "I suppose not. But Jewel's the only one I've ever had over, and she just loves to make fun of everything. And, well..."

"That's hard, isn't it?"

"Yeah. I mean, I know it shouldn't be a big deal. My mom works really hard at her job, and she tries to make this place nice. I should be grateful. But sometimes I just want to run away. Isn't that awful?"

I laughed. "I think God must've made us like that on purpose."

"Huh?"

"Well, we're almost old enough to live away from home, and it seems like the closer it gets, the more ready we are—like young birdies ready to ditch the old nest."

"I suppose." She sipped her Coke.

"How old is your mom?" I'm not even sure why I asked, but the words were out before I had a chance to stop them.

"Well, she's not actually my mom." Anna lowered her voice as if the walls were listening. "She's really my grandma, but my mom left me with her when I was a baby. I've always called her Mom, and she seems just like my mom. But she's sixty-three—a little old to be my mom."

"I bet that's almost how old my mom would've been—I mean, if her baby had lived and grown up to be our age."

Anna nodded. "Well, as much as I love Mom, I have to admit there were times I was embarrassed by her age. I used to wish I had a young mom. Even though Jewel's mom is a real mess, sometimes I'd get jealous of her—they seem pretty close, you know."

"That's probably not so unusual. I'll bet most kids are ashamed of their parents from time to time—no matter how cool or young they appear to be. I know Beanie's been totally humiliated by her mom, like zillions of times."

"At least my mom's never done anything to embarrass me. I mean, she can't help how old she is. And most of the time I don't even think about it. It's only when I'm around other kids. Maybe that's why I've kept to myself so much."

"That's too bad." I set down my empty glass. "Because you've got a lot to offer, and I suspect your mom does too."

She nodded. "Yeah, I've been thinking about inviting her to come to church."

"Oh, you should do that!"

She nodded. "Well, I'll pray about it."

I promised to pray about it too, but then figured I'd better go. "I'd stay longer, Anna," I said as I opened the door. "But you know how it is at my house. I need to help out more right now. But when things get better, I want to come over and meet your mom and everything."

Her eyes lit up. "Great. I've told Mom a lot about you, and she wants to meet you too. She still can't understand why a cool white girl wants to be my friend."

I laughed. "Cool white girl? What made her think that?"

"Oh, I told her you were pretty cool. But I also told her you were nice and that you were a Christian who takes her faith seriously. That seemed to answer her questions—well, mostly anyway."

"Well, I can't wait to meet her now. And I'll be praying that she wants to come to church."

Tuesday, February 26 (yikes!)

Well, we sure had some fireworks tonight. And for a few minutes it got kind of scary too. You see, after the basketball game some of us were just standing around the gym, talking and celebrating our win and waiting for the guys to shower and come out. (Since I had driven Beanie, I had to wait to see if she was riding home with me or Joel.) Then suddenly Natala walks right up to Beanie and just starts laying into her. Of course, everyone's aware that Natala's been in a pretty gnarly mood ever since Jamal broke up with her to start taking out Jewel. (Natala's been calling Jewel the "wetback tramp," which is ridiculous since, according to Anna, Jewel's family has lived in this country for generations.) But anyway, for some reason, Natala sets her sites on poor Beanie tonight.

"What'cha trying to do anyway?" Natala snipes right into Beanie's face. "Who you think you are, missy?"

With wide eyes Beanie tries to step back, but Natala grabs her by the arm.

"Don't you be running from me when I'm talking to you, girl!"

"What is your problem?" asks Beanie, clearly irritated now.

So I step up and stand beside Beanie wondering what's going on and expecting the worst. Jenny's not there because she's working tonight, and when I glance around for Anna, hoping for some support, I realize she's still off at the rest room.

"My problem is that I'm getting a little fed up with these white girls thinking they can move in on our guys."

"Your guys?" Beanie's brows shoot up. "Just who exactly are you talking about, Natala?" A small crowd is starting to gather now, but as I look around I can see that Beanie and I are definitely in the minority here.

"You know who I'm talking about, dimwit. It ain't right you taking one of our best guys from us. Just because you're white, you think you can move right in and take what ain't yours. Well for your information, white don't make right."

Now Beanie blinks, her face a giant question mark. "So are you saying that just because I'm white, I have no right to date Joel?"

"You got that right!"

So Beanie laughs (not her smartest move), and Natala's face tightens into what I would best describe as a snarl, and she jerks Beanie's arm closer to her.

"You think I'm funning with you, girl?"

Beanie quits laughing and shakes her head. "No, Natala. I think you're wrong. And I think you better let go of my arm."

Now I decide to try to help. "Natala," I try to speak calmly, "just let Beanie go, okay? She hasn't done any-thing to—"

"You stay outta this, blondie!"

"Natala," says a girl's voice from the group; I think it was Shonda Newman. "Come on now, girlfriend. You need to just chill out and—"

"You, shut up!" explodes Natala. "It's thanks to sisters like you who keep letting these crackers push us around that makes things stay the way they is. So, you just keep your face outta this!"

"Natala, why do you keep letting color be the dividing

line between us?" asks Beanie in a calm and reasonable voice. "I mean, if you really want things to change you should welcome—"

"I'd welcome you to just shut your face!" Natala's eyes are blazing now, and then (to my horror) she smacks Beanie right across the face with the back of her hand.

"Hey!" I push closer, my adrenaline pumping like pistons, and I grab Natala by her free arm. But I quickly realize this girl has some real muscles. And she gives her arm a fast jerk that sends me flying. And there from my knees, feeling desperate and dumbfounded and slightly humiliated, I look up and see Beanie. I can see her eyes glistening from a blow that must've stung. It's already burning a bright red blotch across her cheek. But it's weird, she's not even reacting or defending herself, but her head's turned as if she's purposely exposing the other side of her face to Natala's next hit! And that's when I realize what's going on. Beanie is turning the other cheek! And I just wait there like I'm frozen in time, wondering what'll happen next and whether I should try to get up and help. And in the same instant I start praying silently, begging God to protect Beanie.

Then suddenly we hear footsteps running and Joel springs into the middle of the circle with Anna just behind him. And like a superhero he grabs Beanie, pulling her away from a surprised Natala. And the crowd actually cheers.

"What's going on here?" he demands, glaring at Natala.

And Natala seems slightly stunned. (I'm not sure whether it's over Beanie's turned cheek or Joel's amazing rescue.) But recovering, she snaps at him. "None of your business, you—you traitor!" Then she turns and stomps away. The other kids stand around and listen and talk for a few minutes as we relay the whole thing to Joel and Anna. And it's amazing how supportive most of them seem to be toward Beanie, saying how Natala's just a hothead and not to worry about her.

It turns out that Anna was just coming back to join us when Natala grabbed Beanie, and suspecting there could be trouble, Anna wisely ran for help. She met Joel coming out of the locker room and told him what was up. I told them I think God was watching out for us.

Beanie rode home with Joel tonight (and now I'm certain she's head over heels in love—I mean, who wouldn't be under the circumstances?). But Anna and I still felt a little shaken by the whole thing and decided to go out and rehash it over mocha milkshakes.

"I can't believe Beanie actually did that," Anna said with real admiration.

"Yeah. I'm sure I wouldn't have thought of that. I'd probably have gotten mad and we'd have ended up in some full-blown, hair-pulling catfight." I shuddered to imagine how horrible and embarrassing that could've been.

"Yeah, me too. And I heard Natala had been drinking underneath the bleachers tonight," said Anna. "So it would've been tough to reason with her. Apparently she pulled a stunt just like this last weekend with Jewel, but fortunately some of the Latina girls stepped in and I think Natala got the worst of it. I suppose she thought the odds were in her favor tonight."

"It was just so weird though, Anna." I set down my shake and looked at her. "I mean, it's like suddenly Beanie and I were the minority there tonight, and I wasn't even sure if anyone would step in to help." I shook my head. "Is that how it feels to be—" I stopped myself, a little worried I'd gone too far.

"To be black?" she finished for me. Then Anna shrugged, and a look I'd never noticed before crept across her face. It was a cross between nonchalance and a quietly smoldering anger. "Yeah, I suppose it's something like that for us." Then she looked me straight in the eyes. "Except when you're white you know it's just a temporary thing. When you're black, it's with you for your entire life."

I swallowed hard, slightly smitten by her words, as if this problem might be personally my fault, although I could see no earthly reason why it would be. And then I could tell that tears were filling my eyes. But I knew that would appear childish, even if it was just a delayed reaction from the anxiety I'd felt earlier.

"I'm sorry, Caitlin," she said quickly. "I know that sounded—"

"No, Anna, I want you to feel free to speak your mind with me. That's how it is between good friends." I forced a watery smile. "And don't mind me; I think it's just been a stressful night."

"Yeah, and I'm sure the last week's taken its toll on you too. How's your mom doing?"

I told her that the tests had come back and how Mom's tumor wasn't cancerous after all but how she still seemed blue about the whole thing. "I'm still trying to be helpful and supportive and everything," I explained. "But to be honest, I want to say 'Just snap out of it, Mom.' I know it's selfish, but I want things to go back to the way they used to be. It's my last year at home. I'd like to remember it more happily than this."

Anna made a sympathetic face, and then I felt really stupid. I mean, who knows what her home life is like? Who am I to complain?

I just shook my head. "I guess I need to grow up."

She laughed. "Isn't that what we're trying to do?"

DEAR GOD, I DO WANT TO GROW UP, BUT I HAVE A FEELING I HAVE A LONG, LONG WAYS TO GO. THANK YOU FOR WATCHING OUT FOR US TONIGHT AND FOR MY FRIENDSHIP WITH ANNA. THANK YOU FOR GIVING ME A BRIEF GLIMPSE INTO WHAT IT MUST FEEL LIKE FOR HER SOMETIMES. HELP ME TO BE MORE UNDERSTANDING. AND THANK YOU FOR WHAT YOU DID WITH BEANIE TONIGHT. PLEASE WATCH OVER HER AND KEEP HER SAFE. AMEN.

NINE

Friday, March 1 (stupid me!)

~~Anna and~~ I went to the mall tonight. We both got paid and wanted to celebrate a little. (Although we're both pretty determined to put most of our earnings into savings.) As a result I'm feeling kind of down right now. Not because I'm trying to save my money, but because I feel like I really blew it tonight.

First of all, we'd pigged out on Chinese food (which was perfectly fine), and then we were just sort of window-shopping around (although we made some small purchases like beaded earrings and CDs). And then as we were walking through Nordstrom (just looking!) I saw these "to die for" shoes. (Well, at least that's how I felt at the moment.) And this good-looking college-aged sales guy hopped right over and started schmoozing and saying how cool they would look on me and how he was sure they had my size, but that these shoes were so hot that this particular pair might not be around for much longer. And the next thing I knew, I was trying them on and Anna was saying how great they looked and how I should splurge and get them, and I was totally hooked. So I plunked down the money (way, way too much!), and the sales guy asked if I wanted to wear them out, and like a dope I said, "Sure" and walked out of the store with a new pair of shoes and an empty pocketbook.

And now (although I didn't tell Anna this) I feel absolutely miserable. I mean, like how did that happen? I've never, ever, not in my entire life, paid that much money for anything—and these are just shoes! Shoes that'll probably be totally out of style by summer. And the money I wasted (yes, wasted!) on these stupid shoes probably could've fed a dozen Mexican kids for a month! Oh, I feel so totally moronic. And, of course, I can't take the shoes back—because I've already worn them! Oh, stupid, stupid, stupid!

Okay, I know it's not the end of the world, and as usual I may be overreacting a little. But it really makes me feel sick in my stomach to consider what I did tonight. Here I've been praying that God will help me to grow up and become more mature, and then there I go and do something totally senseless and self-ish and too stupid. Not only that, but now I think I absolutely hate those stupid shoes! I'll probably never even wear them.

DEAR GOD, FORGIVE ME! I KNOW BUYING SHOES
ISN'T A SIN. BUT AT THE SAME TIME, I KNOW THAT

WHAT I DID TONIGHT WAS WRONG—WRONG FOR ME
ANYWAY. IT WAS WASTEFUL AND IRRESPONSIBLE
AND I FEEL TOTALLY HORRIBLE. PLEASE, HELP ME
TO FIGURE THINGS OUT BETTER NEXT TIME. NOW
I REALIZE THAT YOU FORGIVE ME (AS ALWAYS). I
GUESS I JUST NEED TO FORGIVE MYSELF TOO.
PLEASE HELP ME TO DO THAT. AMEN.

Sunday, March 3 (a welcome revelation!)

At church today, Pastor Tony talked about this ancient
prayer that's hidden somewhere in the Old Testament.
This guy named Jabez prayed the prayer and his life
was dramatically changed. Anyway, Tony taught from
this little book called The Prayer of Jabez (written by
some Bible dude named Bruce Wilkinson), and after
church Anna and I decided to drop by the mall and get
our own copies. And I read the whole thing today and it
was totally amazing. I mean, it's just like God was speaking right to me (especially after my crazy shoe-buying
episode on Friday). And now I feel so absolutely relieved—
it's like I can't even describe it. But I'll try.

   You see, this Jabez guy asks God "to bless him." And I
have to admit that at first that sounded kind of selfish to me. I mean, when I think about praying to be
blessed, I usually think I should be praying for other
people—like my family or friends or the kids down in
Mexico. I never think about asking God to "bless me,
Caitlin O'Conner." Even as I write these words, it still
sounds sort of self-centered and maybe even greedy!

But what this little book so clearly teaches is that we need to realize that God is our loving, heavenly Father and He is so incredibly mighty and powerful and has totally unlimited resources and He can do whatever He wants—and most of all, He just wants to bless His children. Now of course, that doesn't mean that He wants us all to become millionaires and drive Maseratis, but He does want us all to have whatever it is we need to do what He is calling us to do. But first of all we've got to just ask Him.

There's more to this little prayer too. But asking God to bless us is the beginning. And I suppose it's that crazy shoe-buying angst biz that really drives this whole thing home for me. I mean, I'm still not saying it was okay for me to pay that much money for a stupid pair of shoes, but the truth is, the reason I got totally freaked was because I get so worried about whether I'll have enough money for college and to help the Mexican children. (And I'd really like to make another trip down there this summer, whether our youth group decides to go again or not...) Anyway, it's almost as if I was thinking it was all up to little old me to do these things. Like I'm the only one who can provide for my needs. Now how stupid is that? Because think about it: God owns everything (all the mountains and the silver and gold and diamonds and trees and horses), and He can give me absolutely anything. And for me to be down here just beating myself senseless over finances is really kind of ludicrous (don't you love that word?). And even though I don't totally understand all this yet, it just feels like a great, big, giant sigh of relief. Ahhhh...

DEAR GOD, THANK YOU SOOOO MUCH FOR SHOWING ME THIS BIG LITTLE PRAYER. AND FROM NOW ON, I PLAN TO PRAY THE JABEZ PRAYER EVERY DAY. IT'S NOT LIKE I BELIEVE IT'S SOME KIND OF LUCKY CHARM. BUT I THINK IT'LL REMIND ME OF JUST HOW BIG YOU REALLY ARE AND HOW YOU WANT TO BE GIVING ME ALL THAT I NEED AS WELL AS CALLING THE SHOTS IN MY LIFE. SO HERE GOES (IN MY OWN WORDS):

BLESS ME, LORD—PLEASE, BLESS ME A LOT!

AND PLEASE EXPAND MY TERRITORY (HELP ME MAKE NEW FRIENDS).

AND ALWAYS, ALWAYS KEEP YOUR HAND ON ME.

AND HELP ME NOT TO SIN SO THAT I DON'T HURT ANYONE (OR MYSELF). AMEN!

Wednesday, March 6 (moms...)

Mom's doing a lot better now. Almost like before, and I'm pretty sure it's not an act either. She'll go back to work next week—just half days. But I'm feeling relieved that things might get back to normal now. Yet even as I'm feeling relieved about my own mom, I feel a little concerned about Beanie's mom, Lynn. And I'll be praying really hard for her all week.

For the past few months, Lynn had really made some progress. She'd been going to AA and holding down her job, and for the first time since I've known her was acting like a normal grown-up is supposed to act. (Well, at least how I figure they're supposed to act.) But for some reason, she just slipped back into her old habit the other day. Beanie said she got stinking drunk during her lunch break and went in to work and made a complete fool of herself. Fortunately Steph was nearby and took Lynn home and according to Beanie had a long heart-to-heart talk with her.

Beanie thinks Lynn's main problem is that she hasn't really given her heart to God yet. But Steph encouraged Lynn to come to church again and told her all about how messed up her own life had been just a couple years ago. And luckily, Lynn didn't lose her job, but she did get a warning. And because of all this, Beanie was actually considering moving back home—thinking she could help. And this kind of threw Jenny for a loop because she's not real eager to live alone. In fact, she even asked if I'd consider moving in with her. I told her I'd think about it, but after what my mom (and family) has been through lately, I'd kinda like to stick around. Besides, I'll probably be away at college next year. And even though we don't always get along so great, I do love my family and want to be with them for a while longer. So I'll probably have to tell Jenny no. I'm not sure whether it's such a good idea for Beanie to move back with Lynn, but then it's not really my decision, so I'm keeping my concerns to myself. Besides, I've been amazed at how spiritually strong Beanie has gotten in the last six months, so who knows.

Maybe she'd be a good influence on her mom. Anyway, I'm praying that all these things will work out for the best.

I'm still praying the Jabez prayer, and I can tell that it's making me feel more relaxed about the future. It's like I'm starting to believe for some really big things. I mean, why couldn't God just pour all kinds of money into my Mexican dump ministry idea? I remember how cool it was when we came back last summer, and everyone was really generous. And that's continued, but it seems that each month there is less (like it's dwindling away). So now I'm cooking up some ideas for fund-raising and getting the word out. Even though my ideas aren't really big or promising, I believe God can bless them and make them into something way bigger than I could ever do on my own. So it's kind of exciting!

Saturday, March 9 (changes)

I helped Beanie move back home today. And for the first time in a long time, we really spent a lot of time together. But before I go into all that, I must put down a certain new occurrence that's just totally blown me away!

Remember how Jenny was getting kind of freaked about living alone if Beanie decided to go home? Well, right after we heard the news about Beanie's mom falling off the bandwagon, Jenny found out that her parents were splitting up. Apparently Mrs. Lambert discovered that her husband was having another affair. (Jenny said she'd been suspicious since the last time.) Anyway, her mother just sort of flipped out, and as a result her dad left. And Jenny said that after that her mom pretty much had a breakdown. So, what's up with moms these days? It's like they're either getting sick, getting drunk, or going nuts. Well, not really, but it's funny how all three of us have had to deal with mom troubles lately. As a precaution, I asked Anna how her mom was doing (we still haven't met yet), and she said nothing seemed to be out of the ordinary but that she'd be keeping her eye on her—just in case!

Anyway in the midst of flipping out, Mrs. Lambert called Jenny Thursday night and just totally fell apart on the phone, sobbing and swearing and everything! And poor Jenny went home to help calm her mother down. And for the first time (since forever, Jenny said), they sat down and really talked—honestly and openly (no masks, no games). Afterward Jenny agreed to move back home, but only under certain conditions. And her mom was so broken up that she actually agreed to everything. And so Jenny has been home ever since! And she says so far it's going okay and her mom's doing better.

Jenny thinks the reason her mom had been so hard on her before (back when Jenny had anorexia) was because she was so freaked out over her husband's unpredictable behavior. (She'd suspected he was messing around back then too.) And Jenny thinks her mom was just trying to keep everything in their home under control—which proved absolutely useless in the long run. But here's the clincher (something only God could do!): Mrs.

Lambert actually agreed to attend church with Jenny (that was one of Jenny's conditions). Pretty funny, huh? First, Mrs. Lambert wouldn't even allow Jenny to go to church, and then just six months later, she agrees to go to church with Jenny. Now really, only God could do something like that. And so it's entirely possible that both Jenny's and Beanie's moms might actually be at church this Sunday. Although Beanie said she's not holding her breath.

Anyway back to Beanie. After we got her all moved in (and I must say Lynn's a much better housekeeper these days), we went out for coffee and had a nice long talk. I could tell something was bugging her—something besides moving back in with her mom. It turned out to be Joel.

"He's really a great guy," she told me over mochas. "But I think I'm going to have to break it off."

I asked her why and she explained that the more time they spent alone, the more carried away it seemed things were getting—physically.

"You've probably just going to say 'I told you so.'" She eyed me cautiously, her head tipped down.

I shook my head and wiped a finger through the whipped cream and licked it off. "Nope."

"Well, I won't hold it against you."

"Sorry, but I'm not even going there." I grinned at her but kept my mouth shut. (See, I have learned a thing or two lately.)

"Anyway, as much as I like him, I don't think it's doing either of us any good to keep going like this." She sighed deeply. "I don't want it to end up like it was with Zach where we both just hated each other for a long time. And I sure don't want to take any chances getting pregnant. Besides, I made a promise to God, and right now it feels like I'm seriously flirting with danger."

I nodded, still unable to comment (it's like God had my tongue!).

"We were supposed to go out tonight, but I'm going to call up and cancel. I plan to explain the whole thing to him, but I'm worried..."

"Worried?"

"Well, lately we've been taking a little heat...for being a mixed couple, you know. And I don't want him to think that's why I'm breaking up."

"But you're going to explain everything."

"Yeah, but I can tell he's sensitive about the whole thing. I mean, sometimes he even acts like he's inferior or something—which just totally blows me away. If anyone is inferior in this relationship, it'd be me."

"Why's that?"

"Well, for one thing Joel probably has the highest GPA in the school—a solid four-point with hard classes. And he comes from a good family—I mean, they remind me of the old reruns of the Cosbys. His dad teaches at the community college and his mom is an RN. His two older brothers are both in good colleges; the oldest one's about to graduate with a doctorate!" She wrinkled up her nose. "And me, well, I'm just poor white trash."

"Oh, Beanie—"

"I know his mother doesn't like me at all, and his dad's only polite because he's such a nice guy. I'm sure they'll be totally relieved to hear the news."

"But Joel won't."

Beanie shrugged. "Oh, he'll have plenty of other girls chasing after him."

"Like Natala?" I raised my brows, curious to see if Beanie would react.

"Joel wouldn't have anything to do with someone like her."

"Yeah, I know. And for his sake, I hope he'll just chill a while. Maybe you guys can just be friends."

Beanie laughed. "Yeah, you know how much guys like to hear that kind of talk."

I smiled. "Yeah, I remember when I told Josh that. But you know it's worked out over time. We still are good friends."

Beanie looked hopeful. "I wish that would happen with Joel and me. You know it's still awkward between me and Zach, not that we ever see each other anymore. But just those few times we did, well, it never felt quite right."

"Do you guys ever write anymore?"

"Not since around Christmas when he told me he was seeing another girl. I guess I took that as a hint that we were history."

"That's too bad. It would've been nice if you could still be friends."

"Well, it's not that we're enemies. But I just think it's best we let ourselves part ways."

"So were you pretty sad when you heard that?"

"I suppose. I probably wore Jenny's ears out whining about it for a few days—you were gone at that missions conference then. But when Joel asked me out, I sort of just pushed old Zach aside. And to be honest, I haven't really thought about him much since then."

"Kind of a rebound romance?"

Beanie frowned. "No, I don't think so. I really do like Joel—a lot. In fact, part of me can't believe I'm actually breaking up." She shook her head. "But the stronger part—the part that's sold-out for God—won't let me not." She downed the last of her mocha. "And so that's what I get to do when I get home."

I told her I'd pray for her—that it'd all go well. And I have been. I was kind of hoping she'd call, but she might just need to work this out on her own (between her and God, I mean). It's funny thinking of Beanie and Jenny both living back home again. Before they seemed so old and independent. Now they seem more like regular girls—like me. Beanie and I agreed to stop by every day to check on my grandma's cats and things. But it's only for a couple more weeks. So I guess this is all for the best.

tEN

Well, talk about a lose-lose situation. I mean,
when Beanie was going out with Joel she had a few kids
(the Natala types) giving her grief just because they
were a "mixed couple." So she splits with him and now a
few kids are giving her a hard time for breaking Joel's
heart. But I must admit that Joel seems like a shadow of
his former self these days. At first I thought it might be
because basketball season is over (and I think he
enjoyed the limelight a little). But now I honestly think it's
because he really had it bad for Beanie (which is actually kind of sweet because usually guys act all tough
about stuff like that). I asked Beanie if this made her
feel good (I mean, in a bad sort of way), and she got
really ticked at me. I guess I deserved it. Then she told
me in no uncertain terms that breaking up with Joel had
made her absolutely miserable and if it weren't for God,
she'd be back with him right now. But then she lightened

up and said that despite feeling totally crummy for Joel's sake, she knows this whole thing was good for her. And she thinks she learned some good things and has grown a lot too. Now personally, I'm pretty sure I'd prefer a less painful way to grow. But who's to say what's best for someone else? And I didn't want to discourage her.

"I think you've grown a lot, Beanie," I assured her, probably hoping to get back into her good graces. "I mean, honestly, I've been totally amazed by you—especially lately."

She looked at me like I was pulling her leg. "You're serious?"

I nodded. "Like how about that night when Natala laid into you. Man, Anna and I talked about that whole scene for a long time afterward. We were so impressed by your self-control."

"Well, did I ever tell you that Natala actually apologized to me last week? I guess you could call it an apology." Beanie frowned. "I mean, she made it perfectly clear that she was only sorry for hitting me, but that she still stood by her opposition to my relationship with Joel."

"Yeah, and now she's giving you grief for breaking his heart. Kinda flaky if you ask me."

Beanie shrugged. "Yeah, sometimes you just can't win."

"Well, don't let it get you down. I know that God is proud of you."

By then it was time for us to go to a college recruiting meeting that I'd talked her into signing up for last week. It was for this small private college a couple hundred miles from here that we'd never really heard much about before, but we figured if it got us out of history, hey, why not? As it turned out we were the only two there. Kind of embarrassing, but we sure got a lot of attention. And the funny thing is, we were both really impressed with what we heard, and it turned out the college is a Christian liberal arts school. The woman representing the college seemed really interested in us (of course, that's her job), but she even invited us to an open house for potential students during spring break, which is next week. (If we go we can actually stay on campus and see what it's really like.) I was getting pretty interested, but then Beanie cut straight to the point with the lady, explaining how she had hardly anything saved up for college and even though she might get a small academic scholarship at graduation, she felt certain she'd never be able to afford tuition at a private school.

"The truth is, I'll be doing well to afford community college," Beanie said frowning. "And my mom can't help me at all."

"Yeah, and I was figuring maybe I'd head for the state university," I added, as reality set in.

But then the woman told us all about their generous scholarship program (which she felt certain we both had the grades to qualify for), and she explained how we might be able to get a financial aid package plus supplement with on-campus jobs to cover the rest of our expenses. Suddenly we're both thinking maybe it could

happen after all! And as we walked back to class, I told
Beanie all about the Jabez prayer (she'd had to work
the Sunday when Tony preached on it), and I told her I'd
lend her my book because it seemed to directly apply to
this whole college dilemma.

"Because God can afford any college," I told her.
"And if He wants us to go to an expensive, private school,
well then He'll have to get us the funding—somehow. But
if we just assume it costs too much and don't even
bother to ask, well then we'll never really know."

Beanie's really interested both in this college and
the Jabez prayer now. (I plan to give her the book tomorrow.) But the thing is, I'm thinking it could be that God
set this whole thing up for us on purpose, and maybe He
does want us to go to a Christian college together. I
mean, who knows? It could happen. And for the first time
in long time I'm feeling pretty excited about going to
college. Now isn't that weird?

I told Anna all about the college on the way to work,
and then she started getting really interested too. So I
came home and e-mailed the college and asked them to
send all their brochures and things to Anna. I'm thinking
it'd be so cool if the three of us could go there
together—maybe even share a room. But why stop with
three? Maybe Jenny'd like to come too! The idea of doing
something like this sounds so totally cool right now. And it's
funny because it seems like not that long ago I thought
college would just be a waste of time because I wanted
to be a missionary. Now I'm thinking it's probably just

another step toward getting where God wants me to go—
but it might be a fun step at that!

DEAR GOD, THANKS FOR GIVING ME ALL THIS HOPE
FOR WHAT LIES AHEAD. I KNOW YOU WILL GUIDE ME,
BUT I ALSO REALIZE I NEED TO PUT SOME EFFORT
INTO THINGS AND GET MY APPLICATIONS IN. SO,
PLEASE HELP ME TO DO MY BEST. AND THEN I PRAY
THAT YOU'LL EITHER OPEN OR CLOSE THESE
DOORS I'M KNOCKING ON. I TRUST YOU TO LEAD
ME TO WHERE I NEED TO GO TO SCHOOL NEXT
YEAR. AND PLEASE HELP BEANIE AND ANNA AND
JENNY TOO. PLUS, IT'D BE PRETTY COOL IF THE
FOUR OF US ENDED UP AT THE SAME PLACE! AMEN.

Friday, March 15 (big plans for spring break)
Well, it's all settled. The four of us (Beanie, Anna, Jenny,
and me) are all going to visit the campus next week. Anna
and I had to get Monday and Tuesday off from work,
but we think it'll be worth it. We leave on Sunday and I'll
drive. My parents were sort of glad that I was getting so
interested in college, but I could tell they were concerned that it would probably be too expensive. My dad
mentioned my puny college fund several times, like he
was trying to give me a hint. I'm sure they're all worried
that I'll get my hopes up and end up being disappointed.
But I reminded them of the Jabez prayer and how God is
big enough to do anything, and that seemed to quiet
them down for the time being.

Now, here's a bit of news that I'm supposed to keep under my hat but has really got me wondering. It seems that Joel has suddenly taken an interest in Anna! She told me this on our way home from work tonight, making me promise not to tell anyone (especially Beanie). Apparently Joel's been calling her lately (first because he was lonely and missing Beanie), but now she's really hoping he'll ask her out before too long. She says they mostly just talk about what God's doing in their lives, and he told her about how hurt he was when Beanie broke up with him. But according to Anna, he understands Beanie's reasoning and respects her for it. And I suppose that's what has me wondering. I mean, if Joel understands why Beanie broke up (and respects her for it), then why does he (seemingly) want to jump into another dating relationship with Anna? And what's the big hurry?

I know, I know, it's none of my business. But Anna is my friend. And for that matter Joel is too. But I really don't want to see Anna get hurt. She's never really dated before, and she seems to be kind of vulnerable. I mean, she reminds me of Beanie in that way—she's never had a dad. Even though she acts tough sometimes, she's really pretty insecure, and I know how much it would mean to her to have a guy (especially a cool, smart guy like Joel) really like her. I wanted to warn her or something, but then I remembered how badly I blew it with Beanie and Jenny in this area, and I hate to do the same thing all over again with Anna. So I guess I'll just bide my time and pray for her and see what happens next. Still, keeping this news from Beanie won't be easy. Man, I wish we could all just be friends and hang together without this stupid dating thing always messing people up.

Yeah, here I go being all judgmental again! And to be fair, it actually seems that Jenny and Trent are doing okay these days. They don't seem terribly serious and they only go out occasionally, plus they don't even seem to be as clingy as they did right at first. I mean, a lot of couples are totally inseparable these days, like they're joined at the hip and would die if they had to be apart. But Trent and Jenny seem more mature lately. They kind of come and go—like they're giving each other space. And I've noticed they're not so touchy and kissy anymore either. It's like they're handling their relationship in a more grown-up way. And fortunately Trent still comes to youth group sometimes, and he still seems mildly interested in finding out more about God. But at the same time, it's like he keeps this distance too. In a way, he's kind of mysterious. But I keep praying that he'll discover God for himself and give up his silly atheistic beliefs altogether.

It's funny because ever since I discovered that I can't really talk to Beanie and Jenny (and now maybe even Anna) about my concerns over dating and this whole girl-guy relationship thing, it's become the major topic of conversation in my e-mail with Josh. But he still seems really interested and understands how it can be pretty frustrating. And he usually has something helpful to say. Other than that Anita girl he took to the Valentine's Day dance, he's been avoiding dating altogether too. Although he does admit to doing things in groups with girls and occasionally having coffee with a girl just to chat—but nothing serious. And now I'm thinking that sounds pretty good and makes sense. I mean, I hardly think God wants me to just completely avoid the opposite sex altogether—like they've got cooties or something. Now that would be pretty weird. So I'm trying to be more open-minded about these things. And while I know I don't want to get involved in any serious dating, I think I could lighten up a little too. Maybe that's what Jenny and Beanie were trying to tell me a few months back. But I suppose I was just too zealous to listen. Anyway, it feels like I'm growing up—just a little, maybe. Still, I want to make sure I'm hearing God and not just myself.

DEAR GOD, THANKS FOR HELPING ME TO GROW. PLEASE KEEP ME TUNED INTO YOU—ALWAYS! I KNOW YOU'RE THE ONLY ONE WHO CAN REALLY LEAD ME THROUGH THIS THING CALLED LIFE. AND I WANT YOU TO ALWAYS KEEP YOUR HAND ON ME. PLEASE, WORK THINGS OUT FOR OUR TRIP IN A FEW DAYS. AND IF ANY OF US ARE SUPPOSED TO GO TO COLLEGE THERE, I PRAY THAT YOU'LL JUST SPRING OPEN THOSE DOORS SO WIDE THAT NOTHING CAN CLOSE THEM. AMEN.

Monday, March 18

It's our second day here on campus and I absolutely love it! There are all these really cool old brick buildings (with actual ivy climbing up the walls) and lots of big, old trees and grassy lawns and flowers everywhere. They even have a huge pond where you can rent canoes. And then there's this little town right within walking distance with all these great little shops and delis and coffeehouses. And the campus housing seems pretty nice too, although the rooms are a little small (two to a room), and I'm rooming with Anna right now. (Beanie was a little put out, but I had already promised Anna I would.) And now I'm REALLY praying that God will work everything out so I can come here next fall. I know it's a long shot, but I think God likes long shots. And I'm more than willing to give Him a try. The other girls really love it here too. And I think Jenny's already pretty sure she'll be coming (money's not really an object for her). But knowing that she may be here really makes me want to come even more. (Although I realize that's not enough of a reason to come—but I'm trusting God will lead me.)

We got to go to a concert last night. There's this Christian rock band that goes to college here—they've even made one CD. And they were really good, and man, we had such a blast. It felt like we were grown-ups. I know that sounds silly, but I can safely say it in the privacy of my own diary. I mean, we just hung out as late as we wanted (after the concert we went to the coffee shop) and then walked back to the dorm and sat up and talked even longer before we finally went to bed. Then today we got up and had a tour of the academic side of things (which was equally impressive). I think the two main reasons we all like this place so much is because it's a Christian college and it's small enough that we don't feel completely overwhelmed.

Tuesday, March 19 (loose lips)

What a stressed-out trip home! Three and a half hours in a car with two girls who acted as though they hated each other—or maybe it was me they were feeling so hostile toward. Okay, let me explain. As it turns out, Joel did ask Anna out (apparently he called before we left on Sunday and invited her to go to a movie after we got back), and naturally she agreed. Only today she got all wigged-out when we didn't leave right at three o'clock sharp (as originally planned) because she was afraid we wouldn't make it back in time. As a result she was pushing me to hurry it up a little as I was loading the car. Well, I thought it was only Anna and me out there in the parking lot, so I stupidly said, "Sheesh, Anna, it's not like Joel won't wait a couple minutes—"

"Joel?" echoed Beanie's voice as she shoved her bag into my trunk.

I turned and made what I'm sure must've been a real give-away face. "Uh, no, I mean—"

"Oh, give it up, Cate." Beanie just rolled her eyes at

me. Then she shrugged like she didn't care. "Hey, it's no big deal if Joel wants to take Anna out."

Then Anna glared desperately at me and I didn't know what to say.

"Don't worry about it, Anna," said Beanie real casual-like. "I mean, it's a free country, isn't it? And besides, I'm the one who dumped Joel in the first place." But I could tell by the way she said it she was feeling hurt (and I'd never heard her use the word dump before, at least not in regard to Joel).

I noticed Anna stiffen at Beanie's show of indifference. "Well, you don't have to make it sound as if he's just your old castoff, Beanie." Anna folded her arms across her chest as if bracing herself for Beanie's reaction.

But Beanie just shrugged again. "That's not what I meant. But then again, you might've thought that Joel would have waited just a little. I mean, he seemed so hurt and everything—but then again maybe this is just a rebound romance for him." And she really put the emphasis on rebound.

Well, I could tell right then that Anna really didn't appreciate that little comment, and I didn't especially think it was necessary either. Not to mention it was just a tad bit spiteful on Beanie's part. So trying to avoid further confrontation, I waved to Jenny who was just coming toward us, and then I suggested we get in the car and get going. Jenny was all smiley and hopped right into the front seat, totally unaware as to what had just transpired between Anna and Beanie, who were both still standing outside.

"Hey, you guys don't mind if I ride shotgun, do you?" she asked as she stowed her backpack at her feet. "I mean, I got kinda carsick coming up here in the backseat on Sunday."

Beanie and Anna mumbled something then climbed into the backseat. (I'm sure with a good chilly four feet of space between them.) And Jenny started chattering away about how she'd just run into one of the guys from the band we saw the other night (the drummer) and how they'd exchanged e-mail addresses and planned to stay in touch. I just listened and nodded and began to drive. But before long Jenny noticed how quiet and cool the passengers in the backseat were acting. So she turned around and looked at them.

"Hey, what's up with you two?"

"Jenny, uh, maybe just—" But I got cut off.

"Why shouldn't Jenny be in on this too?" Beanie demanded in a sharp voice. "Let's not keep the big news from her. You see, Jen, as it turns out I barely break up with Joel and Anna here makes the move on—"

"Hey, that's not fair—" I start, but now Anna interrupts me.

"I can defend myself, Caitlin. And for your information, Beanie, it was Joel who put the move on me!"

"Whatever." I could hear the edge of tears in Beanie's voice now, and suddenly I realized how much she must really care about Joel.

"Oh, come on, you guys..." I tried.

"Let them work this out for themselves, Caitlin," said Jenny quietly. "They need to talk this over."

"I have nothing more to say," said Beanie. And I could see her stony profile in the rearview mirror, just staring out the side window. And I was afraid she might be crying now (which I knew she would hate).

"Look, Beanie," said Anna in a softer voice. "I'm really sorry about all this. I didn't mean—"

"Don't be," snapped Beanie. I know how much she hates it when people feel sorry for her. "Really, it's no big deal."

"But I don't want it to come between us—"

"Let it go, Anna." Beanie tried to control her voice. "Look, it's over between me and Joel. Whatever he does now is really none of my business. And I shouldn't have said anything. Okay?" I could tell by the way she said "okay" that she was done talking and didn't want to hear another word about it. So after that I attempted to make small talk with Jenny in the front seat. But it was plain to see that our ride home wasn't going to be anything like the ride there. And it sure wasn't. Finally I just tuned the radio to a Christian rock station, and Jenny turned the sound up loud enough that conversation was pretty much impossible.

I dropped Anna off first, and thankfully Joel wasn't sitting out there in his car waiting for her. I can just imagine how that little scene would make Beanie (and I suppose Anna and Joel) feel. Then I took Jenny home.

After that I invited Beanie out for a cup of coffee hoping we could just talk about it and smooth the whole thing over. But she kept saying everything was okay and that she really didn't want to talk about it anymore. Still, I can tell she's hurting inside. And it makes me feel bad to see her like that. And so, once again, I just have to say that this whole dating thing really makes me mad! As a result I sat down and wrote a long (hopefully not too whiny) e-mail to Josh. I realize it's spring break and he might not even be checking, but it made me feel better to get it off my chest.

DEAR GOD, THANK YOU FOR SPARING ME FROM THE DATING GAME PAIN. I CAN SEE, AS I WATCH MY FRIENDS, HOW TOUGH IT IS TO GIVE YOUR HEART TO A GUY—ONLY TO GET HURT ON DOWN THE LINE. AND EVEN THOUGH I'M THANKFUL TO AVOID THESE THINGS, I PRAY YOU'LL HELP ME NOT TO JUDGE OR PREACH TO MY FRIENDS. I REALIZE THIS IS SOMETHING YOU HAVE TO DEAL WITH THEM PERSONALLY ON. AND MAYBE YOU HAVE REASONS FOR ALLOWING THEM TO DATE. I MEAN, WHO AM I TO KNOW ABOUT SUCH THINGS? BUT I PRAY ESPECIALLY FOR BEANIE TONIGHT. I PRAY THAT YOU WILL COMFORT HER AND SHOW HER THAT YOU'RE PLEASED WITH HER CHOICES. AND I HOPE YOU'LL GIVE HER A GREAT BIG HUG TOO! AMEN.

ELEVEN

Friday, March 22 (surprise visit)

Well, totally out of the blue today, about an hour after lunch, Josh stops by my work and asks if he can buy me a cup of coffee. Well, I try to act like I'm not completely blown away and say, "Sure, that sounds good." (I guess I'd sort of forgotten it's spring break since my last three days of vacation have been spent working full time—earning lots of money for college...) So anyway we walk down the street to DiMarco's and order cappuccinos and strawberry cheesecake and have this friendly little chat. (Rita generously told me to go ahead and take a long break.)

"I got this idea recently," he begins explaining to me as soon as we sit down. "I'd been thinking about those kids in Mexico and praying that God would use me somehow to help them. And it occurred to me that I could organize some kind of fund-raiser at school. I talked to my pastor, and he's eager to help out. So I've got my Bible study guys all working with me on this silent auction."

"What's that?"

Then he explains how they'll all go around and ask businesses to contribute things that they can auction off, with all the proceeds going to the Mexican dump kids.

"Josh, that's so cool!" I say, trying not to reveal how <u>totally</u> impressed I am (but I am!).

"Yeah, and I thought maybe you could share some of your photos from last summer with me. We want to make flyers and posters to get everyone on campus involved in it."

"Sure, maybe I could scan the photos on my dad's scanner for you and then just e-mail them."

"That'd be perfect."

I smile at him now, totally amazed at how far he's come in the last year (well, me too). But I have to admit that part of me (a very self-centered part) was just a little disappointed right then too, because when I first saw him today, I had hoped that he stopped by to see me for purely social reasons. (I know: shallow, shallow, shallow!) But by then I could clearly see that he had a specific goal in mind. Duh. He only stopped by because he needed copies of my photos. And not like that wasn't an excellent reason, but I still felt slightly let down. Okay, I AM human!

But after I recovered from my brief lapse into lame self-pity, my mind's wheels suddenly started turning and I no longer particularly cared that he hadn't come by especially to see me.

"You know, your idea gets me thinking," I told him eagerly. "Maybe I could plan some sort of fund-raiser too."

"Yeah, that'd be great!"

"The youth group is still undecided about going to Mexico again this year. Greg is wondering if it shouldn't be something we do every other year. He's afraid the kids will get burned out."

Josh frowned. "That's too bad."

"Yeah, but I suppose I can see his point—sort of. Still I told him that I might be going on my own anyway."

"Really?"

"Yeah, I've already written the mission about it, and as long as I raise my own support, they said they're totally fine with it. That's pretty much what Alex Little does every summer."

Josh nodded. "I've been thinking about the same thing myself."

"Really?"

"Yeah. But I'm still not sure it's what God wants me to do. So I'm praying about it. I can't tell if it's better for me to just send the money and stay here and work—my dad's got a good job lined up for me this summer—or to use the extra money it'd take to go down there and actually help out again."

Then I told Josh all about the Jabez prayer and how I believed that God could and would provide the funding for whatever it is He wants us to do.

"I've heard about that book." His face looked slightly skeptical. "But it sounds to me like people are just praying that prayer like it's some kind of get-rich-quick scheme. Personally, I'm not into that kind of phony baloney."

Well, I quickly set him straight on that one and then promised to send him a copy of the book next week. "Before you go knocking it, you better read it and then decide for yourself, Josh."

He grinned. "Sounds like you're growing up, Catie."

I rolled my eyes at him. "Yeah, well, it happens to the best of us." Then I told him all about the Christian college we'd visited, and he thought it sounded like a great place. "I can just imagine the four of you girls up there." He laughed. "You'll be tearing the place apart in no time."

"Hey, it's not like we're a bunch of wild women." I scowled at him, feeling a little defensive.

"No, Caitlin, I meant that as a compliment. You're all movers and shakers. And from what I've heard, that college could use a little of that."

"I don't know about that. They seem to be moving and shaking pretty good on their own." And then I told him about the Christian rock concert and how Jenny had been e-mailing the drummer, and Josh seemed suitably impressed. Then I realized it was getting late and I needed to get back to work. I thanked him for stopping by.

"Do you still have that get-together at the church on Saturday nights?" he asked as we stood up.

"Yeah, it's not quite as big as it used to be, but the kids who come are more serious about hearing about God. And we're planning on having some special events to draw bigger crowds now and then."

"I might drop by tomorrow night to check it out. And

Zach's in town for the weekend too. Maybe I'll drag him along—just for old time's sake."

"Is he still dating that girl?"

"I'm not sure. We haven't had much of a chance to talk yet. He's been pretty busy with classes, and he has a part-time job on campus."

I wanted to ask Josh if he'd gotten my latest e-mail (about Beanie breaking up with Joel and feeling hurt), but I figured he hadn't. Still, I hoped that maybe Beanie wouldn't go to the Saturday night group now—if Zach was going to be there, that is. I wasn't sure if her heart could handle it, especially after this recent upset with Joel.

Then as we walked back to the office, Josh told me he was worried about his kid sister Chloe. "She's only fourteen but she's acting like she's twenty."

"To be honest, I barely remember her," I confessed. "But she seemed like a sweet kid."

"She is—underneath it all. But right now she's turning into a little tiger. And the weird thing is my parents don't seem to even care."

"Oh, I'm sure they care."

"Maybe. But I overheard my mom telling Dad that Chloe's just like Caleb."

I'd almost forgotten about Josh's older brother—the one who'd dropped out of college and gotten involved in drugs. "Have you guys heard from him at all?"

"Yeah, actually he's doing better. He called me one night and told me that he's been clean for about six months. He's working as a dishwasher in a restaurant and trying to figure out what to do with his life. My parents have pretty much written him off as a lost cause though."

"That's sad." We were at the office building now.

"Anyway, I know you're real busy, Caitlin, but I was wondering if maybe somehow you could talk to Chloe."

"Talk to her?"

"Yeah, maybe you could kind of befriend her—somehow." He ran his hand through his hair. "I know it's a long shot—she might not even want to listen to you. Although last year when we were going out, Chloe thought you were pretty cool."

I smiled. "Well, I'll pray about it, Josh. And I'll see what I can do."

He smiled now, and it was just like the sun had come out. I mean, I'd almost forgotten just how dazzling Josh's smile could be. And suddenly I was really thankful (okay, I was having mixed feelings), but the mature side of me was truly thankful that he was going to school in another town—where the temptation to be with him was greatly alleviated.

Saturday, March 23 (a nice night)

To my initial discomfort, Beanie _did_ go to the fellowship group last night. (Jenny had to work—she still works at the Pizza Hut despite the fact that her mom gives her money for whatever.) And anyway Josh _did_ show up with Zach in tow, and I <u>did</u> feel uncomfortably nervous (for Beanie's sake). I mean, there was Anna with Joel (acting very much like a couple!), and I thought now all Beanie needed was to hear Zach going on about his new girlfriend. But as it turned out, Zach had broken it off with his girlfriend over a month ago. And what had first appeared to be a doomed evening turned out to be an absolute blast! Now go figure.

The four of us ended up hanging together like old pals. No pressure. Nothing. Just plain fun. And afterward we met for ice cream and just laughed and joked and acted silly. Like Josh had said, "for old time's sake." It was so totally cool. And I sat there thinking, This is how it's supposed to be. Guys and girls hanging together and having a great time. No one slipping out back to make out. No tears or angry words. No one getting their feelings hurt. Just guys and girls having a good time!

Wednesday, March 27 (small beginnings)
Well, I've been praying for Chloe Miller the past few days, about whether or not I'm actually supposed to do something with her (which I must admit seemed a little farfetched at first since I'm like a senior and she's still in junior high—I mean, I couldn't help wondering if she would think it's totally weird that I want to talk to her). But anyway, I decided to take the plunge tonight and I called her. Fortunately she remembered me, and while I could tell by the sound of her voice that she was puzzled

about why I was calling her, she was polite and agreed to get together with me on Saturday. I was up-front and told her that it was Josh who'd suggested I might call her and that I knew it probably seemed pretty weird. But I also told her that I remember what it felt like to be fourteen and a little worried about what it would be like starting high school the next year. I told her she could just consider this a big sister kind of thing. And although she laughed (slightly cynically), she seemed somewhat open. What we will talk about on Saturday, I have absolutely no idea, but I'm praying that God will lead me. I'll e-mail Josh and ask him to pray for us.

Thursday, March 28 (an idea!)

All week long I've been praying for a fund-raiser idea. (I didn't want to copy Josh and have an auction.) And finally, just today, something hit me. At first I thought it might be a dumb idea—or maybe just childish, like something grade-school kids would do. So I decided to run it by Tony first. It's one thing to look stupid in front of your pastor (who also happens to be your uncle—by marriage), but it's not fun to look stupid in front of your friends. Now, I know we're supposed to be willing to be fools for Christ's sake. And I am. Or at least I think I am. I just want to be sure it's for Christ's sake before I do it. But as it turned out, Tony really loved my idea. And he didn't think it sounded childish at all.

I think the idea is partly a result of our recent focus

on racial reconciliation. Because lately I've been noticing more how many different cultures we have around here. I mean, we have Latinos and Asians at our church. But I also got to thinking how we all come from so many different kinds of ethnic groups. Like my grandpa (on Dad's side) is Irish. And on Mom's side is Scandinavian. And Beanie has a Jewish dad. Tony has Italian roots. And I know that Jenny's mom is of Ukrainian descent. (She has all these really cool eggs and things handed down to her from her ancestors.) And anyway, I thought maybe we could put together some sort of cultural fair where we have booths and food and stuff that kind of celebrates all our differences. I told Tony that maybe we could call it something like "All God's Children" so that people would be reminded that although we're different, we're all brothers and sisters.

Tony totally loved that idea. (Well, at least he said he did—I hope he wasn't just being nice.) He asked me to put all my thoughts down on paper and to ask some of my friends to come to a planning meeting. He's going to invite some adults who could be helpful too. And the plan is to all get together next week and talk about this idea. It's so exciting.

I wanted to e-mail Josh and tell him all about it, but I controlled myself. First, I want to make sure it's a "go." But even more, I really want to pray about it. And I think I need to be careful not to get a big head over this thing. I mean, sure, it's my idea. But if it's a really good idea, then it probably came from God. And so I don't want to go around thinking I'm so smart and special, when really it's God just using me to do His work. And besides, that sounds way better anyway. Because to be perfectly honest, if I thought this whole thing was on my shoulders, I'd probably just crumble under the stress—and who needs that? So I'm trying to keep everything in perspective. Just the same, I really am excited. And I think it's totally cool if God is using me like this!

DEAR GOD, THANKS SO MUCH FOR GIVING ME THIS IDEA. AND I GIVE IT RIGHT BACK TO YOU NOW. AND I ASK THAT YOU WOULD BLESS IT (JUST LIKE IN THE JABEZ PRAYER) AND USE IT TO MAKE YOUR KINGDOM EVEN BIGGER AND BETTER. AND I PRAY THAT WE'LL EARN LOTS AND LOTS OF MONEY TO HELP THE KIDS DOWN IN MEXICO. WHICH REMINDS ME, PLEASE SHOW ME IF I'M SUPPOSED TO GO DOWN TO MEXICO THIS SUMMER OR NOT. SINCE TALKING WITH JOSH, I'VE BEEN QUESTIONING MYSELF ON THIS TOO. AND I ONLY WANT TO GO IF YOU REALLY WANT ME TO GO. SO PLEASE SHOW ME YOUR WILL. THANK YOU SO MUCH, GOD! AMEN.

Friday, March 29 (weird night)

Today at school I suggested we have "girls' night out" tonight, but both Anna and Jenny had dates, so Beanie and I decided to go see a movie by ourselves. When I stopped by to pick up Beanie, she and her mom were in the middle of huge fight. Apparently Lynn was planning to go out with a guy who Beanie cannot stand, and Beanie was really upset. And somehow I got pulled right into the middle of things—which really wasn't pretty.

"Caitlin, do you think kids should tell their parents what to do?" demanded Lynn.

"Well, not exactly..."

"What about when parents are acting like kids?" asked Beanie, her voice still a little loud.

"I don't know..." And that's when I began to silently pray that God would help us out here.

Lynn looked directly at me, trying to get some support, I'm sure. "You know, Rod is really not such a bad guy. He keeps a regular job, pays child support to his ex—"

"And treats you like dirt!" exploded Beanie.

"You know, Lynn," I began carefully because I could tell that she was getting mad, "I'm hardly the one to give advice on dating here."

Now Beanie started laughing. "Wait, Caitlin, I think you should. Go ahead, girlfriend, climb up on that soapbox and let 'er rip!"

I saw Lynn's eyebrows pop up, like she was bracing herself.

"Okay, look, you guys, you know that I don't think it's such a hot idea to date. But I can only speak for myself. I can't tell you what to do."

"Oh, sure," said Beanie. "Now she holds back on me."

"Well, I'm a grown woman," said Lynn, chest out and hands on hips. "Not a little high school girl. I know how to take care of myself."

Beanie groaned. "Yeah, sure, Mom. Tell me another one."

Suddenly an idea hit me—maybe it was from God, or maybe I'd read it in a book somewhere, but right now I can call it nothing but inspired! "Hey, Lynn," I said as I stepped between the two of them. "Would you marry this Rod guy?"

Lynn laughed. "I may be stupid but I'm not crazy."

I pointed my finger in the air (just like Inspector Gadget). "Well, if you wouldn't marry him, then why would you want to waste your time going out with him?"

I could tell I had her thinking now, but she didn't answer.

"And so what if you're wasting your time going out with this—this loser, according to Beanie, and what if your Mr. Right is out there somewhere just waiting for you to wise up?" I peered into her face. "I mean, have you ever thought about that?"

She frowned. "Not exactly."

Now Beanie stepped in, her voice much gentler this time. "Mom, you've told me that you want God to direct your life, right?"

Lynn nodded, glancing at her watch nervously.

"Well, do you think God wants you going out with Rod?"

Lynn tightly closed her eyes and pressed her lips together, then finally said, "No. Probably not." Then she sank onto the couch and sighed. "But what am I supposed to do now? He'll be here any minute."

"Do you want us to hang around until he gets here?" I offered.

"Yeah, Mom, we could be your moral support."

So we stuck around until Rod (who honestly did seem a little bit like a loser to me too, although I'm trying not to judge) came and honked his horn. Then Beanie offered to run out and tell him that Lynn couldn't make it tonight (which suited Lynn just fine). I'm not sure what else Beanie told him, but hopefully she wasn't too hard on the poor guy. Then we invited Lynn to go to the movie with us, and we all had a great time. Girls' night out after all!

DEAR GOD, PLEASE HELP LYNN TO LISTEN TO YOUR VOICE. I CAN SEE SHE'S TRYING, BUT I KNOW SHE'S GOT A LOT OF STUFF TO DEAL WITH. PLEASE MAKE HER STRONG AND TEACH HER TO TRUST YOU WITH ALL PARTS OF HER LIFE. AMEN!

TWELVE

Saturday, March 30 (oh, man!)

Well, I picked up Chloe this afternoon to take her to the mall (most girls like to go there). But I wasn't prepared for the girl who answered the door. The last time I saw Chloe she was wearing her soccer uniform with her long brown hair pulled back in a neat ponytail—like the all-American girl, right? Well, the girl I picked up today had a spiky, butch haircut (dyed jet black with bleached tips) and a pierced belly button, not to mention numerous piercings in her ears. Her pants were riding so low I was afraid we'd see the moon rising before the sun went down. And her T-shirt (which could've been cute if it hadn't been ripped down the front and several sizes too small) looked like it had never seen the inside of a washing machine.

I couldn't believe Josh's parents (who I'd thought were fairly conservative, church-going type people) would let her out of the house like that. But I tried really hard to be totally cool, not acting the least surprised. I mean, I see kids like this all the time at school, and it's not like it's some great big deal, but to see Josh's kid sister like that— Well, it kind of blew me away, I guess. And I can understand Josh's concern now.

Chloe and I walked around the mall for a while, and it was quickly obvious that our taste in fashion differed greatly, although I've had some experience here (with Beanie) so I tried to just chill and be a good sport. And I think she was surprised that I wasn't being all critical of the stuff she liked. Then we stopped to get a snack and I decided to just cut to the chase.

"I'm sure you're probably thinking it's pretty weird for me to want to spend time with you," I began.

She kind of shrugged and took a loud sip on her soda. "Whatever turns you on."

I laughed. "Well, like I said, Josh really cares about you, and he thought we'd like to get to know each other."

"You mean he wants you to take me on as some kind of pet project—like, "Let's do a makeover on Chloe" or something equally lame. Like you guys think you're playing Pygmalion or something."

"You know about Pygmalion?"

She shrugged again. "Yeah, you know, like My Fair Lady—you find the most socially objectionable person and you try to remake them into something acceptable and totally boring."

I felt my brows shoot up. Chloe was no average fourteen-year-old girl. "No, no," I kind of stammered. "That's not what this is about—"

"Then what IS it about?" she demanded, thunking her drink cup down.

"I'm not even sure," I said. "But I think Josh felt like you could use a friend."

"I have friends."

"I mean someone older."

She rolled her eyes. "I have parents."

"Yeah, I know. But sometimes parents can be pretty thick."

"You're telling me."

"And I know you're going into high school next year and that can be kind of scary."

She narrowed her eyes. "I'm not scared."

"Okay, maybe scared was the wrong word. But it's like everything is changing—and sometimes things can change real fast—and then there's friends and boyfriends and it can get rough."

I thought I saw her face soften just then. But she didn't say anything.

"Do you have a boyfriend, Chloe?"

Her expression grew hard again. "What do you care?"

Okay, now I was praying silently, feeling like I was in way over my head with this fourteen-year-old. "Well, I could be wrong, but I'm thinking you've been hurt, and maybe by a guy."

She looked slightly curious. "What makes you think that?"

"Just intuition, I guess."

She shrugged again then leaned back, tipping her

chair onto two legs as she plunked a heavy Doc Marten boot onto the small table. "Everybody gets hurt, you know."

"Yeah, I know. I've been hurt too."

She rolled her eyes again, but I could tell there was some interest flickering there too. "Did my brother hurt you?"

"Yep. He pretty much broke my heart once."

"But you guys are still friends?"

I smiled. "Well, I kind of broke his heart too. At least that's what he said. But you might not want to repeat that to anyone."

"So are you guys back together again?"

"Not as in dating. But like you said, we're still friends."

Now she looked slightly puzzled.

"Do you want to talk about the guy who broke your heart? You can trust me not to repeat anything."

She removed her boot from the table, leaned forward, and proceeded to spill out a story that almost made me cry (but I controlled myself). Apparently she'd had a severe crush on a certain popular boy throughout junior high. And finally in eighth grade (after he'd gone through numerous girlfriends), this boy actually noticed her. Before long they started "dating" (which mostly means they hung out together since he didn't drive or anything). But the relationship quickly became pretty serious, and after just a couple of weeks, he started pressuring Chloe to have sex with him. And though she was a virgin (and only fourteen!), she was eager to keep him and wanted to prove she was "really mature," and so she agreed. But when the actual time came, she got kind of upset and scared, and suddenly she backed out (which made him really mad!). And the next day, he broke up with her in school, but not until he told everyone that they'd "done it." (She thinks it was so he'd look like the big stud.) And suddenly her friends started treating her differently, and she was so depressed about the whole thing that she started pulling away from her so-called friends.

"I haven't told anyone what really happened," she finished, her eyes slightly misty but hard as stone. "Mostly because I doubt if they'd believe me anyway. And after what Andy said, I know they all think I'm a slut. Even my best friend—well, she used to be my best friend."

I reached over and put my hand on her arm. "Thanks for telling me all this, Chloe. It's so unfair."

She took in a deep breath then sat up straight, kind of defiant-like. "Yeah, but that's life, isn't it? I mean, we're supposed to get kicked around a little—used and abused, you know. It's just the way it goes."

I shook my head. "It doesn't have to go like that."

"Well, if you don't experience pain, then how do you know you're really alive?"

"I don't mean that life will ever be pain-free. I know mine sure isn't. But last year I gave my life to God, and now when I experience pain it's not as bad as it used to be. I mean, it's not like I'm going through everything all on my own anymore, you know? It's like I have someone to talk to—someone who cares and can make a difference."

"You actually talk to God?"

I nodded. "All the time."

"Do you really think He's listening?"

"I do. I'm certain of it."

She started fiddling with her cup, tearing the top into little jagged spikes. "Well, I still believe in God, at least I think I do. But I don't go to church with my parents anymore. Actually I think they've relieved. I'm pretty sure they're embarrassed by me." She stuck out her chin. "And I don't give a rip. Because I happen to like the way I look."

"Is that because it keeps people at a distance?"

I could see a little bit of a smirk sneaking onto her lips. "Maybe..."

"So do you feel safer this way?"

"Maybe...sometimes anyway."

"You mentioned someone who used to be your best friend?"

"Yeah. Jessie—she was a real, true friend! I mean, as soon as I started acting different she started pulling away. And then when I started changing the way I look, man, she just took off running the other direction like I was contagious with herpes or something."

Then I told Chloe about Beanie, and how that had been a little trying for me sometimes, but we'd weathered it, and I was really thankful for her friendship now. She seemed to appreciate that.

"I remember when Beanie dyed her hair bright blue," I told her, suppressing giggles. "But after a few days, she didn't really like how it looked, but even so she didn't want to change it back—she was afraid everyone would think she'd wimped out. So she just left it blue for about a month or so."

"Then what?"

"I think she put a reddish color on next, but then it ended up looking like fuchsia."

Chloe laughed. "I'll bet it was cool."

Then we talked some more, and I realized it was getting late and I'd promised Mom that I'd be home in time for dinner. I asked Chloe if she wanted to do this again sometime and she said sure, and I'm pretty certain she meant it.

"Call or e-mail me anytime you want to talk," I told her as I dropped her off.

"You sure?"

"Of course, I wouldn't say it if I didn't mean it."

Then she thanked me—and I could tell it was sincere.

DEAR GOD, PLEASE HELP CHLOE TO SEE THAT YOU LOVE HER—JUST THE WAY SHE IS. PLEASE SHOW HER THAT YOUR WAY IS THE BEST WAY AND HELP HER TO GIVE HER HEART TO YOU. AND USE ME IN ANY WAY YOU CAN TO ENCOURAGE HER. I CAN SEE SHE'S REALLY A NEAT KID (AND SMART TOO). I JUST WANT HER TO KNOW HOW MUCH YOU LOVE HER! AMEN.

Wednesday, April 3 (progress...)

All right! The fair's all set. Well, almost anyway. We still have a lot of details to tie down. But we had our first meeting tonight (about a dozen of us and the official planning committee), and everyone voted unanimously to call it All God's Children. We'll have it on Saturday, May 25. Martha Anderson (who's on city council) is going to see if we can hold the event at the park. And Tony suggested we might even invite the other churches in town to participate.

Even though I strongly protested, they all voted and decided that I was to be chairman of the committee. I must admit that I'm pleased to do it. I just hope I can do a good job. I mean, I have work and graduation isn't too far away and—oh, I'll just have to pray that God helps me to make good choices. And like Martha pointed out, just because I'm the chairman doesn't mean I have to do all the work. There are lots of people willing to help out. She was already making a list of businesses to ask to sponsor booths and things. It was exciting hearing everyone throw out ideas and stuff. If we can do even half the things we talked about, the fair should be a huge success.

No one had any problem with the proceeds going to the kids in Mexico. Although Tony suggested that perhaps this might become a yearly event and maybe a new group could be selected each year to benefit from the proceeds. Steph agreed, saying that would probably help other churches to get involved too, since they might have specific ministries they'd like to help out—and it would be more democratic. And so, it's all set. And I'm so excited.

DEAR GOD, THANKS FOR PULLING THIS WHOLE THING TOGETHER. I PRAY YOU KEEP IT GOING SMOOTHLY AND HELP US WORK OUT ALL THE DETAILS. AND HELP ME TO BE A GOOD CHAIRMAN AND MAKE GOOD DECISIONS. LIVING LIFE FOR YOU IS SO EXCITING, GOD. I CAN'T IMAGINE HOW BOR-ING MY LIFE WOULD BE WITHOUT YOU! THANKS FOR LEADING ME. I PRAY THAT I'LL ALWAYS, ALWAYS FOL-LOW YOU. AMEN!

Thursday, April 4 (down and out)

Chloe called me up tonight, and I could tell by the flat sound of her voice that she was depressed. She's really feeling out of it at school—alone, picked on, a misfit... And while I wanted to tell her that it might be her own doing, I just couldn't bring myself to say those words (besides, she must know). So I mostly listened for a long time, and then I finally told her that what I think she's really longing for is a relationship with God. I told her how Jesus died so that she could be forgiven and have a relationship with God. She listened but didn't respond. Then I told her I could remember exactly how she felt, because it wasn't that long ago when I was there too, but I also said that without God we'll always be lonely (whether we're on the inside or the outside or somewhere

in between). I told her that I loved her and cared about
her and that I'd be praying for her. I told her that I
believed God had really great things in store for her,
and that this was just His way of getting her there. I
think she might've been crying by then, but she covered
it up pretty well. Finally, she said she had homework to do
and hung up. And I've been praying for her off and on all
night.

I e-mailed Josh, and without telling him everything
(out of respect for Chloe), I let him know that she was
really struggling now and could use a lot of prayer. I also
plan on inviting my friends to pray for her too.

Friday, April 5 (some opposition)

It seems like things for the fair are still falling pretty
much into place. Although Steph told me that one particular church in town doesn't like the idea of a cultural fair and are actually trying to put a stop to it.
Now, what's up with that? I mean, what's not to like
about it? But Steph said not to worry about them. She
said Tony told her that just because people are
Christians doesn't mean they always see things the
same way. There are bound to be churches that don't
agree, but that probably can't really put a stop to the
fair. I hope not. I'll be praying that God will work this
thing out. Although I'll admit it's hard not to feel really
irked and totally dislike that church (Steph wouldn't
tell me which one it is), but I keep reminding myself

that God loves all of us, no matter what, even when we don't agree. So I'll try to keep my attitude under control.

Lately, I've been thumbing through the mail pile every evening, hoping that I'll find an acceptance letter from the Christian college, but so far nothing. I suppose it's too soon. But I've heard other seniors at school have gotten acceptance letters—of course, they might've sent their applications in sooner too. The other girls haven't heard anything yet either, which is something of a relief. And Beanie and Anna seem to have patched things up. Beanie is even managing to maintain a friendship with Joel these days. (Although Anna admitted to me, just tonight on the way home from work, that this bothers her some and she feels guilty and stupid for feeling jealous.) I didn't make many comments and tried to act sympathetic, but at the same time I was thinking, Yeah, sure, well that's what comes from getting all romantically involved with a guy when you're still in high school. Like what do you expect? But thankfully I kept these thoughts to myself. Now, I suppose if Anna specifically asked me for advice, I might tell her. But I'm pretty sure she (and everyone else) knows where I stand on this issue, and I don't need to go climbing back on my soapbox again.

I finally e-mailed Josh about the cultural fair, and he thinks it's a super idea. But I didn't tell him it was MY idea. And for some reason that made me feel good inside. Why is that? I'm not even sure. But it does. Maybe it's from that Bible verse where Jesus tells us to do our good deeds in secret so that only God can see, and then He can reward us. I'm not totally sure, but it's something I'd have to think about some more. Because I know how I really am deep down inside, and it's not very pretty. The truth is, I really like attention. And I like it when people think I'm really great and that I'm doing good stuff. It's like a big ego trip. But at the same time I know that's not right. And I'd like to change. Maybe I am changing.

DEAR GOD, I'M GLAD THAT YOU CAN SEE WHAT'S REALLY GOING ON INSIDE OF ME—AND THAT IT DOESN'T MAKE YOU GO RUNNING IN THE OPPOSITE DIRECTION. AND I'M REALLY GLAD THAT YOU LOVE ME—NO MATTER WHAT! BUT I DO WANT TO CHANGE. I WANT TO BE MORE LIKE YOU. AND I THINK MAYBE YOU'RE HELPING ME TO CHANGE (ONE TINY STEP AT A TIME). PLEASE HELP ME TO DO GOOD THINGS FOR YOU (AND NOT FOR THE ONLOOKERS). I KNOW I NEED TO LIVE MY LIFE FOR YOUR EYES—AND NOT WORRY SO MUCH ABOUT WHAT OTHERS THINK. BUT I NEED YOUR HELP. AMEN.

THIRTEEN

Tuesday, April 9 (a little bummed)

Okay, now I'm feeling a little bummed.
Jenny just called, all ecstatic, to tell me she got her
acceptance letter from the college today and her mom
says she can go. Well, of course, I acted all thrilled and
excited for her, but at the same time I was really thinking, Hey, where's my letter? Now, I know that sounds totally
selfish and immature, but the truth is, I really wanna go
too! Whaa—whaa—whaaaaa! And I'm just not happy at
all right now.

Okay, Caitlin, get a grip now, girlfriend! Your letter
will be here too. Just take a deep breath now and
chill.

Well, I felt a little better after I called Beanie and
found out she hadn't gotten a letter either. But then
she was sounding all depressed too and I almost wished I
hadn't called. (Although I'm sure it was just a matter of
time before Jenny did anyway—not that I blame her. I'd

probably do the same if I were in her shoes—and I wish I were in her shoes!)

"I probably won't be able to go anyway," said Beanie in a quiet voice.

"You don't know that."

She sighed. "Sometimes you've just got to face reality, Caitlin."

"But God can do anything."

"Yeah, I know…" Beanie's voice sounded pretty sad. "And I believe that, but it just doesn't feel like it right now, you know?"

"Beanie, it sounds like you're feeling pretty low. Is everything okay over there?"

Then she told me that her mom was having a hard time again. "I mean, it's not like she's off getting drunk tonight or anything," she explained. "In fact, she just went to bed 'with a headache,' she said. But she seems all negative about everything right now. She says her life is going nowhere, and that she'll never have a good man, and that she's a crummy person, yada, yada, yada.… And anyway I'm getting kind of worried that she'll go back to her old stuff again. I mean, it's like the writing's on the wall or something."

"Do you want to pray for her right now?" I offered (surprising even myself since I'm still not that comfortable praying where people can hear me). But Beanie agreed and so the two of us prayed together, right over the phone. And it was so cool. Beanie sounded a little better then—more hopeful. I promised to keep praying for Lynn

every day. Before we hung up, I assured Beanie that I
believed God would either open or close the door to that
college for us and that we could totally trust Him—that
He has our absolute best in mind. And that seemed to
make her feel better too. I know I feel better now. I'm
trying not to feel bad (or jealous) that Jenny got her letter first. Also, I just remembered that she didn't have to
apply for any financial aid or anything, so that might've
made it quicker.

Wednesday, April 10 (ray of hope)

Chloe called again tonight and she sounded better. She
thanked me for talking with her last week and said
she'd been thinking about what I'd said but still wasn't
too sure about it. Then she got real quiet. To keep the
conversation going, I started telling her all about the cultural fair we're planning, and she was really interested. I
invited her to help, and she seemed genuinely eager to
be involved and wants to come to our next planning meeting. I'm not sure what the church folk will think when
they see her clothes and multiple piercings, but then I
guess we'll just deal with it at the time. Maybe they'll
have to ask themselves, What would Jesus do? However, I
know Tony and Steph will be fine with her, and that's
reassuring.

Chloe told me that her mom's side of the family is
Dutch and that she has a collection of things that her
grandma brought her after a trip to Holland. I asked if

she wanted to think about doing a Dutch booth, and she suggested maybe she could sell tulip bouquets, which I told her was absolutely brilliant. So she's going to be looking into that possibility. I really like Chloe and am truly starting to think of her as a little sister. I just hope that she realizes ASAP how much God loves her. It's so hard watching people struggle.

Speaking of struggles, Jenny mentioned that Trent has been kind of depressed lately. She's not really sure why, but she asked us to pray for him. And so we all are. Personally, I think he's depressed because he's trying to live his life pretending that God doesn't exist. Sheesh, that would depress anyone! He still comes to youth group occasionally, but he doesn't seem to get any closer to making a commitment. I actually think (although I wouldn't admit this to anyone) that the only reason he comes is to keep Jenny. I can tell he really likes her, but I'm not sure she's as serious about him. And come to think of it, I suppose that could be depressing him too. Maybe he's afraid he's going to lose her. Well, who knows? Just the same I'll be praying hard. Man, my prayer list just gets longer and longer!

DEAR GOD, I'M SURE YOU'RE AT WORK IN TRENT'S LIFE RIGHT NOW. I PRAY THAT YOU'LL OPEN HIS EYES TO SEE YOUR HAND ON HIM. SHOW HIM HOW MUCH YOU LOVE HIM AND HOW MUCH YOU WANT TO HAVE A RELATIONSHIP WITH HIM. I KNOW IT MUST BE LONELY FOR HIM TRYING TO LIVE HIS LIFE ALL

ON HIS OWN LIKE THAT. PLEASE WIN HIM OVER FOR
YOU. IF THERE'S ANYTHING I CAN DO TO HELP HIM,
PLEASE SHOW ME WHAT IT IS. AMEN.

Thursday, April 11 (seriously bummed!)

Okay, now I'm feeling really out of it. Both Beanie and
Anna have gotten their acceptance letters. And they
both got these incredible financial aid packages and
good scholarships with the promise of on-campus jobs. I
mean, it's like totally amazing! Both of them are flying
high right now. And I put on this really great little act,
saying how cool it was and how great that God has done
this amazing thing—yada, yada, yada—blah, blah,
blah....

I guess I really do feel that way—I mean, I am truly
happy for them. But at the same time I feel bummed
and really left out. And it was hard not to just break
down and cry right there in the cafeteria (which would
be totally lame). While I was at work today, I almost
called the college to see what was up. But then I told
myself to just chill—be patient. I know that good things
are worth waiting for. And my letter is probably in the
mail right now.

Still, it's hard and I feel like it's unfair. I mean, I'm
the one who was first interested in that college, and I
helped get everyone else all involved, and now I have to
be the last one to hear. And yet, I feel pretty certain I'll
be accepted. My GPA is a little higher than Jenny's and
Anna's (not Beanie's though). And I did write a pretty

good essay (if I do say so myself, plus I did win that writing award last year). So anyway, I guess I need to chill out and trust that God knows what He's doing. And just now I'm remembering a certain Bible verse that tells us to be glad when we get tested (and that's what this feels like) because our faith gets stronger with each test. So tonight I'll go to sleep believing that my letter will be here soon and that God has everything under control. Ahh, I feel better already.

DEAR GOD, THANK YOU FOR HOLDING MY LIFE IN YOUR HAND. AND HELP ME NOT TO GET ALL BUMMED JUST BECAUSE MY SILLY LETTER HASN'T COME YET. I TRUST YOU WITH THIS WHOLE COLLEGE BIZ. I KNOW YOU HAVE MY BEST INTERESTS AT HEART. FORGIVE ME FOR GETTING SO WORKED UP ABOUT EVERYTHING. AMEN.

Friday, April 12 (woe is me)

Well, my acceptance letter arrived today. And at first I was jumping up and down ecstatic to read it—because the first line said "Congratulations, you've been accepted..." But as I read more carefully, I quickly realized that I was getting absolutely no financial aid— zippo, nothing, nada! (Apparently my parents make just enough money not to qualify!) And while I did get a nice little scholarship package, I didn't think it was enough to cover the difference. Still I decided to check with my parents just in case.

Anyway, at dinner tonight, I announced that I'd been accepted and then raised the money issue, explaining how I didn't qualify for any financial aid. And that's when Dad said that's how it goes with a lot of families these days. "I know lots of parents who make too much money to get financial aid but not enough to afford private school tuition." And then he (nicely) assured me that we certainly couldn't afford that kind of tuition either. "I sure wish we could, Caitlin," he said apologetically. "And I'm sorry we didn't put away more money for your college earlier on. But at least we put away some. And I know you can go to the university with no problem whatsoever. We can cover that."

"I know you're disappointed, honey," my mom said in this sweet, tentative voice, like she thought I was going to start blubbering like a baby or something. "But remember it's not like you won't be able to go to school at all. At least you've still got the university, and it's a great school. You know, Dad and I both went there."

"I know." I forked into my salad, determined not to actually cry in front of my family (especially my brother Benjamin). I wanted to appear mature and grown-up about the whole thing.

"And I know it must be hard to see your friends all going there," began my mom. "But you know their circumstances are different. Jenny's folks are wealthy, and well, Beanie and Anna are in perfect situations to get really good financial aid, and—"

"Let's not talk about it anymore," I said, trying to

swallow a bite of salad over the lump growing steadily larger in my throat.

Then my dad jumped in again, trying to put a positive spin on the whole thing. "Maybe God has a reason for having you go to the university—"

"I just don't want to talk about it." But it was too late now. The tears were already streaming down my face. "Excuse me!" I blurted. And then (yes, just like a baby) I ran up to my room and threw myself across the bed and sobbed. Pretty silly, huh? But I just feel so let down. I mean, I was believing in some really big things from God. I was telling my friends to believe big things too. And now this! I feel so humiliated. It's like God ripped the rug right out from under me! And it just doesn't feel fair!!!

DEAR GOD, WHY HAVE YOU DONE THIS? I THOUGHT YOU WANTED TO BLESS ME IN A REAL BIG WAY! NOW, IT FEELS LIKE YOU DON'T CARE ABOUT ME AT ALL. MAYBE YOU LOVE BEANIE AND ANNA AND JENNY MORE THAN ME. BECAUSE THAT'S WHAT IT FEELS LIKE RIGHT NOW. FORGIVE ME IF I'M WRONG FOR GOING ON LIKE THIS, BUT I KNOW YOU'LL UNDERSTAND. AND I'M A LITTLE BIT MAD RIGHT NOW. PLEASE HELP ME GET THROUGH THIS. AMEN!

Saturday, April 13 (encouraging friends)

At least I have the weekend to recover from my disappointment. I finally called my friends and told them the sad news, and they were all totally sympathetic and couldn't believe it. Beanie actually said she wouldn't go if I couldn't go, but I told her she HAD to go. Her only other real option would be community college, and the private college would be soooo much better. She said she'd think about it, but I could tell she was really upset (and I suppose that made me feel better—a real friend should be upset).

Then to my surprise they all three showed up at my door tonight (it was about nine) and kidnapped me and took me out for ice cream. (They bought me a triple-decker with hot fudge and caramel sauce.) And there we all sat, talking and crying, and I could tell they were all almost as unhappy as I was that I wouldn't be going. And even though it still hurts deep down inside, I guess I feel just a little bit better. Still, it's like I've been hit by a truck or something. I mean, I feel so totally disoriented now. Like I had this great plan and then poof—it all just disappears! I keep telling myself that God has a plan for me, and that there's a reason for this disappointment, but to be honest I can't see it.

When I got home, Dad was still up reading the paper, and he asked me if I'd sent in my application to the university.

"Well, I didn't really think I'd be going..."

He cleared his throat. "But, Catie, I told you last winter that you needed to get it in. Right here in the paper is an article about how enrollment is higher than ever right now, and it's not that easy to get in."

I groaned and sank down into the chair across from

him. "Maybe this means I'm supposed to go work in Mexico, Dad. I mean, that's what I originally wanted to do anyway."

He sighed loudly. "But I thought you said the people at that missions conference said you needed to get your college degree first."

"Well, what am I supposed to do now?"

"Probably get your application in to the university. And to be safe, I guess you'd better apply to the community college too."

I leaned back into the chair and closed my eyes, suddenly feeling totally worn out by all of this—college, life, decisions, everything. "I just wish I could be a little girl again."

Then Dad came over and put his arm around my shoulder. "You'll always be my little girl, Catie."

I had to smile at that. "Thanks, Dad."

It's times like tonight that I feel sorry for girls who don't have a dad to say something like that to them. But then I have to remind myself that God is their Daddy. And I know He's my Daddy too. But right now I'm just not too sure what my heavenly Daddy is up to.

DEAR GOD, PLEASE HELP ME TO TRUST YOU—EVEN WHEN IT FEELS LIKE YOU'VE TOTALLY FORGOTTEN ME. I'M SURE YOU HAVEN'T. AMEN.

Sunday, April 14 (some encouragement)

Well, I spent the afternoon filling out applications for both the university and the community college. And although it's just totally depressing to think I may end up at the community college—I mean, that's the place NO ONE wants to go, the place that kids make fun of at school— I'm trying to believe God has a reason for all this. And even if I have to go there (for a semester or two until I can transfer), I'll just have to make the best of it.

I suppose it helped me to hear Tony's sermon today. (I wondered if my mom didn't tell Steph what was up, and she told Tony, and... There I go thinking the entire universe revolves around ME again!) No, it was probably just one of God's magnificent coinky-dinks that Tony preached about "humbling yourself beneath God's mighty hand, so that in due time He could exalt you...." And I have to admit that I can't think of anything quite as humbling as Caitlin O'Conner (honor student) being forced to attend community college with all those less fortunate people (and lots of older, down-and-outer sorts go there too).

Now, I'm sure that sounds really superior and proud (but a diary is so forgiving), and it's the humiliating truth. And maybe that's just the reason God could be sending me there (to knock me down a peg or two). Or maybe He has something even better in mind. Maybe He'll use me to touch some lives—people who are really struggling.

I'm suddenly reminded of the Mexican kids at the dump and how I had been so appalled by them at first. I mean, I didn't even want to touch them or have them touch me. And then what happened? I got so attached to them that I didn't want to leave. I think about them and pray for them and work to make things better.... So, anyway, who knows? Maybe this is just the way I am. I'm all opposed to something, and then it turns out to be the best thing ever. Well, I'm really trying to see it that way. Time will tell though.

DEAR GOD, THANKS FOR USING TONY'S SERMON TO IMPROVE MY ATTITUDE. I STILL DON'T KNOW WHAT YOU HAVE IN MIND FOR ME, BUT I'M TRUSTING THAT ALL IS WELL AND YOU HAVEN'T FORGOTTEN ME. TEACH ME TO BE HUMBLE AND PATIENT WHEN YOU DO THINGS I DON'T UNDERSTAND. HELP ME TO KNOW THAT IN TIME YOU'LL MAKE EVERYTHING PLAIN AND CLEAR. AMEN.

FOURTEEN

Wednesday, April 17 (honest confession)

Well, it's time for me to come completely clean about all this college biz. And I hope as I begin to write stuff down it'll all start to make more sense. Because when I first realized that the private Christian college was out of the question, I naturally assumed I'd be going to the state university (which would thrill my parents but not me particularly).

My primary concern was: That's where Josh goes to school. Now, on one hand, that should make me totally happy. Right? Wrong. (Okay, it does make me a little bit happy.) But mostly it just makes me pretty worried. Why? Okay, here's the tough part... It's because I don't entirely trust myself. There, I've said it. Phew. It's just that I'm worried that my feelings for Josh are intense enough that if he and I were living on the same campus (with a whole lot less supervision than at home)—who knows? I mean, it seems likely that we might start seeing each

other, maybe regularly. (Oh, we probably wouldn't call it
dating, but then what would we call it?) And even though
we both say we're against getting seriously involved—well,
what if we did? And what if things got too hot and
heavy and I was tempted to, well, say, break my vow to
God? Oh, this is almost too humiliating to actually write
about—but at the same time, I think it's a moment of
truth for me. Because the fact is, this whole thing worries me. I worry me. And Josh worries me. And yet at the
same time I honestly can't imagine anything more fun
that being on campus and hanging with Josh. Pretty sad,
isn't it? Not to mention confusing. I mean, I'm starting to
feel like the "double-minded man" that the Bible
describes as a wave—just being tossed all over the place
by the wind. And I think I'm starting to feel seasick! Look
out! Woman overboard!

   Sheesh, I'm not even sure if I know what I'm talking
about just now. I guess the main thing is I feel frustrated
and confused about my future. And I'm thinking why
would God want to put me in this position? I mean, that's
one of the main reasons I wanted to go to the Christian
college in the first place—it sounded so safe and
secure—a good place for someone like me. And so for all
of the reasons I've just stated, I suppose I'm secretly hoping I'll get stuck at the dumb community college next
year. Even if it does sound totally depressing. And naturally, I can't let my parents know about this. So for their
sakes, I'm pretending that I hope to get into State (which
makes me feel like a hypocrite). Because deep down, I

suspect I'll be better off closer to home. Not that that makes me feel any better. Mostly I feel like a flaky college reject who doesn't even know her own heart or where she wants to be next year. I just feel kinda mixed up and lost today.

DEAR GOD, I'M SORRY TO BE SO PITIFUL ABOUT ALL THIS. BUT I GUESS I JUST NEEDED TO SAY THE TRUTH. AND FRANKLY I DON'T EVEN FEEL MUCH BETTER HAVING SAID IT. IT'S LIKE I'M LOSING SIGHT OF WHO I AM OR WHAT I'M ABOUT. I THINK MY SELF-ESTEEM WENT DOWN THE TOILET THE DAY I REALIZED I WOULDN'T BE GOING OFF TO SCHOOL WITH MY BUDDIES. AND NOW IT SEEMS ALL I DO IS WHINE AND COMPLAIN TO YOU ALL THE TIME. I'M REALLY SORRY. PLEASE FORGIVE ME. AND PLEASE HOLD MY HAND. I CONFESS I'M FEELING PRETTY SCARED AND LONELY JUST NOW. HELP ME TO TRUST YOU WITH EVERYTHING—ALL PARTS OF MY LIFE. I PUT IT ALL IN YOUR HANDS. AMEN.

Saturday, April 20 (nothing's wasted)

We had a really great planning meeting today for the cultural fair. Chloe came with me, and while she got a couple of strange looks (from some of the older, more conservative members), everyone was generally nice to her. Our committee has grown to about thirty people (with numerous other churches sending representatives). And fortunately for me, Martha has offered to cochair the group (which is a huge relief since she's really good at getting people to listen and stay on the subject).

Anyway, things really seem to be falling into place there, and despite that one particular church's opposition, we've managed to secure the park for our event. The opposing church had written a letter to the city saying that it was wrong for a "church function to be held in a public place." But apparently the city was unimpressed by their letter, and so it's all set.

Already offers of donations from local merchants have been coming in, and I'm hoping that we'll really raise a lot of money for the Mexican kids. One of the first things I did was to design posters and flyers (describing the fund-raising event as well as where the proceeds were going). My dad helped (since he's the advertising pro) and the company I work for threw in all the materials and printing. I shared the posters and flyers with everyone at the meeting tonight, and they were all pretty impressed with the quality. Which, I must admit, made me feel good. And while I know I should focus on pleasing God (not people), it's still pretty nice when someone appreciates your work. And I think it's good timing too (considering my recent identity crisis). Perhaps God just wanted to use this to encourage me. Anyway, I'm feeling a little better.

But here's what was really cool about tonight. As I drove Chloe home she was being kind of quiet, so I just jumped in and told her a little about how low I'd been feeling about this whole college thing (well, not the part about her brother but how it had been getting me down some). Anyway, I think it really helped her to see me in a different way.

"And here I thought you had it so together," she said as I pulled into her driveway.

I forced a laugh. "Hardly."

"Well, it's not like I'm glad you've been miserable," she said as she opened the door, "but it does give me hope."

"Glad my pain and suffering can be of service." I smiled.

"So did having God really make any difference then?"

"Oh yeah. I honestly don't know what I'd do without Him."

She seemed to be considering this as she climbed from the car. Then she thanked me and headed toward the house, her hair still standing out in rebellious little spikes (kind of like a mad porcupine). And although her pants were still riding revealingly low, there was this slight spring in her step that I hadn't noticed the previous time. And I prayed for her as I drove home.

Then I sat down at my computer and e-mailed Josh about her, reminding him to pray. And this time I decided to tell him that there was just the slightest chance I'd be coming to the university in the fall. I only briefly described my disappointment about not getting to go to the Christian college (I'm really trying to move on). And mostly I just wanted to hear his reaction to the possibility of us attending the same school next year. Not that he should really care that much one way or the other. But I guess I'm just curious.

Tuesday, April 23 (cracking the shell)

I was eating lunch with Anna and Joel today (Beanie and Jenny were at another table that was already full) when Natala came and flopped down right beside me, which was fine with me (although somewhat surprising since she makes no secret of her general dislike of "crackers" as she calls us of paler skin tone). So anyway I turned and smiled and said, "Hey."

She gave me what I might best describe as a withering look (I think Jane Austen uses that description sometimes). Then she said, "What're you doing over here polluting our table?"

"Oh, lay off, Natala," said Joel (which I appreciated).

And feeling emboldened by his defense, I decided to speak up. "Natala, why do you always seem to hate me so much?"

"Honey, I don't hate you," she said condescendingly. "I don't even know you. And fact is, I don't want to know you. I just wish you'd stay where you belong."

"Where do you think I belong?"

She nodded over to a predominately white table. "With your own kind."

Now Anna jumped in. "You know, Natala, it's people like you who keep things just the way the are."

"People like me?" Natala exploded. "It's people like your

little white cracker friend here—people who've kept us in
our place for years—people who wipe their big white feet
on us—they're the ones that keep us back and hold us
down—"

"Natala, you don't even know what you're talking
about," said Joel. "Can't you hear yourself? You're making
a personal case over a really bad generalization and
then taking out all your aggressions on Caitlin. It's not only
stupid, it's wrong."

"Watch who you be calling stupid, stupid!" Right then
Natala reminded me of an angry cat with her ears back
and her claws out.

"Natala," I tried to use a calm voice. "I just wish you
could chill long enough to see if we couldn't become
friends."

"You and me?" she asked, and her face looked like
I'd just suggested she should go eat dirt or something.
"Listen, girl, the day you and me become friends is the
day I see pigs fly."

I just shook my head, finished my lunch, and left. I'm
not sure why, but something about what she said had
cut right through me. I mean, I realized that her words
were untrue, but just the fact that she felt compelled
to speak them made me really sad. Like I was wondering,
how did we get to this place? Why can't the divisions
between everyone just dry up and blow away? I suppose I
was still thinking these things as I stood in front of the
sink slowly washing my hands. But when I looked up into
the mirror, I suddenly realized that Natala was standing

next to me (not close but a couple feet away), and she was just staring at me as if trying to size me up.

She squeezed her brows together then finally spoke. "You mean what you're saying in there, back at the lunch table?"

I studied her for a moment, unsure as to her motives (and even wondering if she was considering beating me up since it was only the two of us in the bathroom just then). "Yeah, Natala, I meant what I said. I just wish you'd give me a chance. Maybe you'd find out that we're really not that different after all."

Now she threw back her head and laughed, but it was a cynical laugh and I was getting worried. Then just as quickly she sobered and stared back into the mirror again. "Look at us, girl!" She pointed to our reflections (and I must admit my hair looked blonder than ever, my eyes a washed-out shade of blue—it was kinda scary really). "You honestly think we're not so different? Well, I think you're nuts. Certifiable even."

"Color is only skin deep, Natala. You peel it away and we'd look just alike underneath."

"Yeah, we'd look like something out of a Freddy Krueger movie."

Now this made me laugh. "Yeah, I suppose we would." But I could tell she was almost smiling now too. "Look, I know you've probably got a hundred reasons to dislike white people, Natala."

"Make that a million and you'd be closer."

"Okay, how about a bizillion then? But the thing is, you

don't really know me or any other white person—not really. And I just wish you were willing to get to know us— one person at a time—before you made up your mind about everyone."

She held her head high. "And what if you're no different? What if you're just like all the rest of them I'm-better-'n-you white crackers that go around walking all over folks? What then, Miz Caitlin O'Conner?"

"Well, then at least you'll know what you're talking about. But I'm betting you'll be surprised."

She rolled her eyes. "So what are you suggesting? You think maybe you and me should get all cozy and sweet? You want me to start calling you girlfriend?"

I smiled. "Not unless you want to." Then I thought for a moment. "Hey, how about this? How about if we go hang out at the mall together this Friday night? If you're not busy, that is. If you want I can even pick you up—or we can just meet—whatever. Maybe Anna or Jenny or Beanie could come too. And you could bring some of your friends if you want. Maybe Shonda would like to come."

She just kept looking at me, as if she didn't really trust me. "I'll think about it."

I smiled at her again. "Good. Let me know, okay?"

And so I'm feeling slightly hopeful that maybe, just maybe, we'll actually make some progress here. I suspect that underneath all that hardness, Natala is hurting inside. I'm sure she needs God way more than she could possibly realize. And I'm going to be praying for her for the rest of the week.

Friday, April 26 (breakthrough!)

I hadn't seen much of Natala the past couple days, but today she stopped me in the hallway and told me that she and some friends would meet me at the mall—at the food court at seven. "And if you don't show—"

"Don't worry, Natala, I'll be there. Really."

Beanie had to work tonight and Anna already had a date with Joel, but Jenny agreed to come. We thought we might just visit with the girls for an hour or so and then maybe see if they want to take in a movie that's just released. (It's kind of a childish movie, but Jenny and I wanted to see it anyway.) As it turned out, it was only Natala and Shonda who showed up, and I could tell by their expressions they already had their defenses up—as if they expected us to do something totally lame.

But to our relief, after a few minutes, everyone started to loosen up a little (and I must give Jenny most of the credit here; she was fantastic at cracking jokes and getting everyone to just chill). And once Natala and Shonda relaxed, we realized that these girls were a whole lot of fun. I mean, some of their jokes were a little on the raunchy side and their language wasn't exactly "church-friendly" (after all, they're not Christians), but for the most part they were a total hoot. And I think we all had a really good time. But when Jenny and I told them about the movie, they thought we were messing with them.

"That's a kiddy flick," said Shonda, rolling her eyes

as she touched up her lip gloss.

"We know," I began. "But we thought it'd be fun."

Natala shook her head. "Well, I, for one, am sure not wasting my money on that stupid movie."

"Hey, how about if we treat?" suggested Jenny.

"Yeah," I agreed. "And that way if you don't like it, you won't be out anything."

Natala narrowed her eyes. "You chicks serious? You want to take us to the movies? What's up with that?"

"It'd be fun. Why not?" Jenny checked her watch. "It's almost time. You guys coming?"

Shonda looked at Natala then shrugged. "Sure, if you want to waste your money on a stupid kids' movie. We'll come along."

So the four of us went to see a kiddy movie. Piled high with our tubs of buttery popcorn, Reese's Pieces, and giant-sized sodas, we all trooped in and sat down with a bunch of wiggly grade-schoolers and their parents and watched a goofy movie about a neurotic dog who wanted to save the world. And when it was all said and done, both Shonda and Natala were surprised at how much they enjoyed it, and Jenny and I tried not to appear overly smug.

"See," I gently jabbed Natala in the arm as we left, "you shouldn't judge a book by its cover."

She made a face. "Well, it's hard not to do something that's been happening to you for your whole life."

Then we piled into my car and went out for coffee and donuts (like we needed more sugar!), and Jenny and

I told them all about the upcoming cultural fair that we're planning. I explained how Joel and Anna are putting together an African-American booth, and they both seemed fairly interested.

"Do you think they need any stuff?" asked Shonda, suddenly catching the vision. "I mean, my dad's got this big old trunk full of things from the sixties—like newspaper clippings and pictures of Martin Luther King, Jr.—you know, from the Civil Rights movement."

"Yeah, you should tell Joel about it. I'll bet he could use some of it."

"My mom was involved in all that too," said Natala in what almost seemed a hostile tone.

"The Civil Rights movement?" asked Jenny as she dunked her jelly roll into her coffee.

"Yeah, I guess she was a teenager then, but she was in a couple of the big marches. One time, I heard her telling my aunt about the time that they got hosed down."

"Hosed down?" asked Jenny.

"Yeah, policemen and firemen were trying to break up the march and they used fire hoses—going full blast. My mom said that it just knocked them right over and stung like heck." Natala glared at us as if we were personally responsible.

"That's so horrible," I said. "I can't even imagine what that must've felt like."

"Yeah, and even though it was a peaceful protest, my mom said the police shot tear gas right into the crowd and used clubs and everything."

I sighed. "Hearing about stuff like that makes me understand why you have some serious hostility and resentment toward white people." I paused for a moment, studying their faces. And then I said something that I hadn't planned, and I wasn't even sure why I said it. It just seemed right. "And, you know, even though I wasn't around when all that crud happened, I'm really, really sorry."

"Yeah, me too," Jenny chimed in.

And it was a weird moment right then, like something even bigger than I could understand had transpired. And both Shonda and Natala kind of nodded and acted like maybe they forgave us (which still seems weird because I know Jenny and I aren't personally responsible). But then we all just sat there, real quiet for a bit.

Then Natala spoke up. "I guess it helps some hearing you say that. I don't know exactly why, but it does." Then she reached up and gave us both a high five. "Now, I'm not promising that I'll always mind my manners around you crackers," she said, with a sparkle in her eye. "I mean ya gotta know that old habits die hard. But I'll try to remember that you're not like the rest of the crackers out there."

And so I suppose that's a start. And to be perfectly honest, I have to admit that I've been almost as judgmental of Natala as she was of me. Oh, not based on her skin color, that's no big deal...but more because of her actions. I mean, she's a real in-your-face sort of girl—the kind I might normally try to avoid. But now I'm seeing that actions aren't all that much different than skin color—because actions don't always reveal what's inside a person. And I can see how girls like Natala and Chloe (and even Beanie back in the old days) use an exterior layer of toughness and hardness and even meanness to hide those tender places that can get hurt deep inside. I suppose it's just a survival skill that they've adopted over the years. I'd probably be more like them—if not for God, that is. I think it's only because of His hand on my life that I'm able to take the pain (and I admit I haven't had a whole lot—not like some people). But when it does come my way, it seems like it's cushioned by God's love, and in time I can even use it to learn from. But without God, I'm sure I'd start building up that same hard, tough shell to protect myself too.

DEAR GOD, PLEASE SEND YOUR LOVE TO NATALA AND SHONDA RIGHT NOW. PLEASE SHOW THEM THAT YOU WANT TO BREAK THROUGH THOSE HARD SHELLS AND REALLY TOUCH THEIR HEARTS WITH WARMTH AND HEALING AND LOVE. AND PLEASE USE ME (AND MY FRIENDS) TO LOVE THESE GIRLS LIKE YOU WOULD, AND HELP THEM TO SEE WHO YOU REALLY ARE. THANK YOU FOR ALL THAT HAPPENED TONIGHT. I PRAY YOU KEEP IT GOING AND GOING AND GOING! AMEN!

FIFTEEN

Wednesday, May 1 (feeling good)

So far this has been a cool week. We've hung out with Natala and Shonda a little more, although Natala still plays tough chick from time to time. I try not to let her hurt my feelings though. And it seems like Shonda is a little more interested in hearing about God. Of course, she acts all sort of mellow and laid-back about it—kind of ho-hum. If Natala is listening, she won't even go there. I'm sure Shonda's trying to protect her tough-girl image. Just the same we've invited both girls (once again) to come to the fellowship on Saturday night. And we tried to make it clear that for the next few weeks we'll be mostly working on things for the cultural fair, so I don't think it should be too intimidating for either of them. Anyway, they said they'd think about it, and I'm betting they'll be there.

On the way home from work tonight, Anna told me that she's worried about Jewel. Apparently Jamal broke up with her this week, and she's really devastated by the whole thing. Anna said she wasn't even at school today, and Anna doesn't think it's because she's sick. Anyway she asked me to pray for her. And without thinking I mentioned to Anna that this is exactly the sort of thing that really bugs me about dating.

"I just hate seeing my friends get all bummed when someone breaks up. I mean, who needs all that heartache?"

"Yeah, well, isn't it just a fact of life?"

"I don't know." I glanced over at her, suddenly remembering she was in a pretty serious relationship and it was only last week that she'd freely admitted to me that she was "really in love with Joel and hoped that they'd get married someday," for Pete's sake! I mean, who really knows who they're going to marry when they're barely out of high school? Okay, maybe some people do. But I just don't get that.

So anyway, for Anna's sake I piped down about the whole thing. And I told her I'd be praying for Jewel, but in reality I'll be praying for her too. Because the truth of the matter is, I feel pretty certain that Joel isn't as committed to their relationship as Anna. He just doesn't seem to look at her the way I remember he used to look at Beanie. And even now, sometimes when Anna's not around, it looks like Joel's flirting with Beanie. And Beanie just acts like they're good friends (because she really does like Joel), but I think Joel is thinking there might be something more there. And it seems highly likely that sooner or later Anna is going to get hurt—and maybe badly. But I guess I should remember that she has God to fall on. I mean, it was only a year ago that Josh dumped me, and in many ways it was that very thing that really solidified my relationship with God. Maybe it's just like that Bible verse says, maybe all things really do work for the good when you love God and try to do what He wants you to do. (Well, that's my own paraphrase, but I think it pretty much says it.) So maybe I should just keep my mouth shut and pray more.

Man, my prayer list is getting long. I used to feel bad sometimes because I was only praying about one sentence (or even less) for each person on my list—either because I was about to fall asleep or else I just couldn't think of anything really great to pray. But then I decided to just pray randomly from my list. Now I sort of read over the names, and when one pops up I pray specifically for that person. Sometimes I just pray the Jabez prayer, but other times it feels like God is leading me to pray something else. But this way everyone gets prayed for eventually. And it's a lot more fun than just feeling like I'm going down the grocery list, saying "God bless Beanie, God bless Jenny...yada, yada...," which really must make God want to take a snooze!

As a result it feels like God is giving me some really cool things to pray for—things I don't think I could've thought of all on my own. And anyway, praying has suddenly become more of an adventure lately. I think I may even start writing down some of the things I'm praying for—just to see if they really happen. But who would've thought that something as simple as prayer could be so cool!

Thursday, May 2 (a sad, hard day)

Today when I got to school I could immediately tell something was wrong. It's like everyone was sort of clustered in these little groups with really sad faces. I spotted Anna by her locker and went over to see what was up and heard the sad news.

Anna turned to me with tears running down her face. "Jewel Garcia tried to commit suicide last night."

"You're kidding?" I felt waves of shock running through me. I mean, I'd actually been praying for her—just last night. "What do you mean 'tried'?"

Anna let out a little sob, and I put my arms around her and hugged her. "Is she alive?" I asked quietly.

Anna stepped back and nodded soberly. "She's in ICU right now, but she might not make it." Then she broke into sobs again, and Natala came up and told me the rest of the story.

"It's all Jamal's fault," she said angrily. "That boy just doesn't know how to break up with a girl. Take it from me—been there, done that! Anyway, Jewel was really torn up about it, and she got a hold of her brother's gun—he's involved in...well, you know—and she just let herself have it right in the head."

I gasped. "But she's alive?"

"Barely. I heard that she didn't aim the gun straight,

and the bullet is lodged in her skull."

I felt my knees getting weak and now tears were fill-ing my eyes too. I leaned into the lockers for support and stared at Natala in wonder. "How can you handle this, Natala? I mean, you don't seem upset or anything."

She rolled her eyes and then shrugged. "It's not any-thing I haven't seen before. My next-door neighbor got shot just sitting in her own living room—a drive-by, you know, wasn't even her fault. You get sort of used to these things." Then she scowled. "But not in your world, I guess."

Then I stood up straighter, suddenly feeling pretty defensive. "You know, Natala, I don't think anyone's exempt from this kind of stuff. I mean, just last year one of my best friends was killed in the McFadden School shooting—Clay Berringer—and I still miss him to this day."

She looked slightly taken aback by my words but simply nodded.

"I'm sorry, Natala," I said. "I guess I'm just really upset." I took in a breath, trying to regain some composure, which seemed pretty futile about then. "The thing is, just last night I was really praying for Jewel." I glanced over to Anna who was still quietly crying. "Anna had asked me to. And, well, I feel really cruddy right now—like my prayers didn't make one bit of difference—" And then I started to cry too. And to my surprise it was Natala who put her arms around me and patted my back.

"Maybe your prayers did make a difference, Caitlin," she whispered. "Maybe that's the reason Jewel's still alive."

I hadn't considered that possibility, and I wasn't entirely convinced right then, but I tried to remember what she said—I tried to hang on to it during the day. Still, I felt pretty unsettled and shaken by the whole thing—not to mention let down. I mean, I wasn't exactly blaming God, because I know He gives us all freedom of choice and everything. But it was hard to think that even though I'd been praying for Jewel, she still pulled that trigger. I just couldn't wrap my mind around it. I wondered why God hadn't done some miracle like making the gun not work or something. I suspected I was looking at this all wrong, but it was just the way I felt. I couldn't even pray.

Then at lunchtime, a bunch of us went together to buy balloons and flowers and then drove over to the hospital to deliver them. We figured they wouldn't let us into ICU, but the nurses were really nice and said they'd let Jewel have our gifts as soon as her condition improved. Anna actually got to see her (through the glass window), and she said it looked like Jewel was still unconscious and was plugged into all kinds of machines, but the head nurse seemed to be hopeful and told us that she would get better in time. Still, I don't know if that's just the way they're supposed to act in ICU, like it's part of their job or something.

Then Anna suggested that we all meet at the hospital this evening to pray for Jewel. And so after work we grabbed some burgers at the take-out window and drove straight over. And when we got there the waiting room was packed full of kids—some Christians, some not. I'd estimate there were about a hundred of us. Earlier today, Joel had invited Greg to come over and sort of lead us all in a prayer vigil. And it was actually pretty cool. I mean, kids who would never consider coming to church were actually bowing their heads, and, I believe, really praying for Jewel.

The crowd started to break up a little before nine, but some of us stayed on (mostly the Christian kids as well as her closest friends), and we continued to pray. We weren't always praying out loud. And mostly we just bowed our heads in silence. But sometimes someone would read something from the Bible. Around midnight, I figured I better get home (since I'd promised Mom I would). And even though I feel totally exhausted, I plan to pray for Jewel during every waking moment. And I'm really believing that God has His hand on her life. And somehow this is all going to work out right.

DEAR GOD, ONCE AGAIN I ASK YOU TO KEEP JEWEL IN YOUR HAND. SOMEHOW, I PRAY YOU WILL SPEAK DIRECTLY TO HER HEART RIGHT NOW AND TELL HER HOW MUCH YOU LOVE HER. PLEASE, DEAR GOD, PLEASE KEEP HER ALIVE! AND PLEASE GIVE HER ANOTHER CHANCE. SHE NEEDS TO KNOW YOU, GOD. SHE NEEDS TO EXPERIENCE HOW MUCH BETTER LIFE IS WITH YOU IN IT. OH, PLEASE HELP HER, I PRAY IN YOUR SON'S NAME. AMEN.

Friday, May 3 (encouraging news)

Anna had news about Jewel this morning. Apparently her condition has stabilized. We're not totally sure what that means, but Anna says it's good. Jewel's still unconscious and in ICU, but if she remains stable they will probably do surgery on her this afternoon. We decided to gather in the lunchroom at noon today to fast and pray for her. The fasting part was Joel's suggestion, and we all agreed. We were willing to do whatever it took to get God's attention, not that we think He's not listening. (Okay, I'll admit I had my doubts yesterday.) But we just want to do anything we can to help Jewel. We started out with about thirty kids, gathered in a corner of the cafeteria, but before lunchtime was over I'd estimate we had more than a hundred—maybe two hundred. It was amazing! And when we finished, Joel led us all in a couple of praise songs. Naturally, most of the kids didn't know the words, but those who did sang loud and clear. And it was totally cool! Joel suggested that we turn tomorrow night's fellowship group into another prayer vigil at the hospital and everyone agreed.

Then Anna called the hospital (late this afternoon) to check on Jewel's condition and found out that the surgery had gone well—even better than expected. They removed the bullet and the damage was less than they originally thought. Still, she hadn't regained consciousness yet. But we're feeling more hopeful—and still praying.

Monday, May 6 (more good news!)

The weekend was full—with several prayer vigils for Jewel plus work on the cultural fair, and as a result I never even had time to write in my diary! But the good news is, Jewel has regained consciousness! The less than good news is that she's sustained some serious brain damage (no big surprise when you consider what she's been through). But according to Anna (who got to visit her tonight), the doctor said it's not nearly as bad as they'd expected. And he thinks she can recover—mostly anyway—but she may never be the same as before. And she'll have to relearn how to do all the simple things like walking and talking and eating—kind of like being a baby again. And Anna said that in a few days they will want people to start visiting her, regularly.

Anna said that Jewel's family (a single mom and two younger brothers) are all pretty overwhelmed by everything and could really use any help they can get (including financial). So I called up Tony and asked if we could put the word out at church and see if people want to donate money to help them out. And Tony asked how I'd feel about seeing some of the funds from the cultural fair going to Jewel's family, the Garcias. And, at first, I felt slightly protective of the Mexican orphan kids, but then I realized how totally selfish that was—and how God is big enough to take care of everyone. So I said, "Sure, but shouldn't the whole committee vote on it?"

"Yeah, but I just wanted to run it by you first, since

this whole thing was your idea to start with."

And so we'll bring it up at the committee meeting this week. I'm thinking they'll probably agree. Because as my grandma has been known to say, Charity begins at home. And I'm thinking if you can't help the people right around you, how can you expect to help those who are far away?

Tuesday, May 7 (no big deal)

Well, I suppose I should feel something, but I don't. I got an acceptance letter from the university today. Mom and Dad were just totally thrilled because they were afraid I'd get stuck at the community college. (And even though they'd tried to pretend that would be okay, I knew they were hoping for better.) The problem is, I was still hoping the university would be full by now. But in light of everything that's gone on lately, I'm thinking, Who cares? I mean, sheesh, I should just be thankful I'm getting to graduate and go to college. Right? When I consider poor Jewel stuck in the hospital and having to relearn everything, well, I should just be thankful. And so I'm not going to worry about it. God must know what He's up to.

Maybe I'm mature enough that I can handle being on the same campus as Josh without totally going to pieces. And right now I'm thinking it's pretty funny how wigged-out I'd been about all that. How totally lame! Still, I wish I could feel a little more enthusiasm about the whole thing. And I'm thinking I would be—if I were going to the Christian college. (I know Jenny and Beanie and Anna are enthused.) So, I guess I'll be like Scarlett O'Hara and just think about all that tomorrow.

Thursday, May 9 (hmmm?)

First, I'm happy to report that the fair committee thought it'd be great to share the proceeds with Jewel's family. In fact, they were so supportive they decided to make it a fifty-fifty split (which I must admit seemed overly generous to me). Okay, I know I'm sounding all self-ish again. And this isn't anything I would tell anyone. But maybe my problem is that I'm just limiting God again. I mean, I should just be praying that He'll really bless the event and raise twice as much money as before. And so that's what I'll do!

On another note, I got an e-mail from Josh today. I had e-mailed him and told him that I'd most likely be going to the university with him in the fall. But you know what he told me?????

He said that he'd applied to go to Bible college and that although he hadn't heard back yet, he believed he'd be accepted—and as a result wouldn't be anywhere near the state university next fall. Well, go figure! Now, I suppose I should be jumping up and down with relief. But to be perfectly honest, I'm feeling a little let down. Now, is that lame or what? I mean, here I've gone on and on about how terrified I am to be "alone and on campus" with Josh Miller (sounds pretty dumb now), but suddenly it's no longer a threat, and I'm disappointed. All

I can say is: Caitlin O'Conner, you are one flaky chick!
But I'll keep that little piece of information to myself
(just in case anyone else out there hasn't already
caught on). Anyway, I e-mailed back to Josh saying how
great it was that he was going to Bible school and how I
was proud of him. And then of course I remembered how
he had mentioned all this at Urbana last winter—how
he might like to become a preacher and all. But like so
many things, I guess it just went in one ear and out the
other. Oh, my...

I didn't say anything about this to Chloe. (She went
to the meeting with me again tonight—we were organiz-
ing booths and stuff.) I figured Josh could tell her (if he
hasn't already). But Chloe and I ended up talking a lot
about what happened to Jewel. I hadn't really seen
Chloe since that whole thing, and she had read about
it in the paper and was naturally curious since half the
proceeds from the fair are going to their family and
all.

"Why did she try to kill herself?" Chloe asked as we
drove from the church to her house.

"Well, I don't know if anyone knows for sure, since she
didn't write a note or anything, but the word is she was
devastated because her boyfriend broke up with her."

"That's what I would've guessed."

"Really?"

"Yeah, that got me pretty down."

"Did you ever consider anything like that?" I glanced
at this little rebel sitting in the passenger seat of my car.

She nodded. "Yeah. Not with a gun though. I would've used pills."

I groaned. "Oh, Chloe, you wouldn't do anything like that now, would you?"

She shrugged. "You never know."

"But just because you go through a time when things look really bleak, don't you realize that it's going to get better?"

"Maybe I do right now, but not when I'm feeling really depressed. Then all I feel is hopeless."

"Would you like to go visit Jewel with me sometime?" I suggested, although I'm not even sure why.

She shrugged again. "I don't know."

"They say she's going to need a lot of visitors to stimulate her and help her to get better. We're making a roster at school so we can take turns seeing her. I'd like it if you wanted to come with me, especially since you're on the fair committee and we're donating half the proceeds." I knew this was kind of a lame excuse on my part, but suddenly it seemed important that Chloe (who still seemed somewhat casual about this whole suicide thing) should come see firsthand what this is really like.

"Okay, I guess I could come."

"Good. I'll call and let you know my time slot."

DEAR GOD, PLEASE KEEP YOUR HAND ON CHLOE. I KNOW YOU'RE DOING SOMETHING IN HER LIFE (EVEN IF I CAN'T SEE IT). PLEASE HELP ME TO BE HER FRIEND—USE ME IN ANY WAY YOU CAN. AND

PLEASE KEEP HELPING JEWEL TO GET BETTER.
AND HELP HER TO COME TO KNOW YOU, LORD.
SHOW BOTH THESE GIRLS HOW MUCH YOU LOVE
THEM. AMEN.

SIXTEEN

Saturday, May 11 (just a year ago...)

At the fellowship tonight, we took
time to remember that exactly one year ago, Clay (and
two others) were shot at McFadden High. Pastor Tony
visited us and spoke briefly about life and death and
violence and God's love. And it was really powerful. For
one thing, we had more kids than ever (a result, I'm sure,
of Jewel's suicide attempt), but the amazing thing was
how everyone seemed so eager to really "hear" the truth
tonight. I mean, so many times we've had the fellowship
group and it's been pretty lighthearted and well, almost
trivial. And I'm not saying that's wrong—in fact, I'm sure it
was absolutely right—almost like it was building this foun-
dation of trust or something.

Anyway, tonight kids were really touched by Tony's
words. (He even asked us to continue praying for the
shooter who was convicted and sentenced as an adult
but has been willing to meet with Tony.) And afterward I

saw a lot of quiet conversations going on between Greg
and Tony and some of the kids who appear to be sin-
cerely searching. But perhaps the most amazing of those
was when Jamal (brought tonight by Joel) asked to speak
to Tony alone. We all could see how much he's been hurting this week. And he hasn't talked to anyone and mostly
just walks around school with his head hanging down.
Even Natala softened up and actually felt sorry for him
this past week, but he wouldn't even talk to her.

But the other incredibly great thing tonight was how
Beanie and I got to talk with Natala and Shonda for a
pretty long time. I think this thing with Jewel has shaken
them up a lot more than they're letting on. And tonight
Natala even admitted that she's afraid of death. She
said she's afraid that if she died she would just cease
to exist—poof—disappear forever.

"And I really do like living," she said. "Oh sure, it's real
hard and all, but I basically like life. And I'm not ready
to just hang it up. But at the same time I don't think I
can do all this goody-goody church girl stuff. It's not my
style, if ya know what I mean."

And so Beanie and I tried to explain about how God's
not looking for a bunch of "goody-goody" people, but how
He just wants us to let Jesus (His Son) into our hearts—to
be our friend and to help us out.

"It's like it's up to God whether or not you need to
make any changes in your life," I tried to explain. "And He
only asks us to change the things that either hurt us or
hurt others."

"And you have to understand He works differently with everyone," said Beanie. "Like my mom. She's a Christian now, but she still smokes cigarettes and cusses and stuff. But that doesn't mean she's not a Christian."

"That's right," I added. "God doesn't expect us to automatically become perfect when we invite Jesus into our lives. He just wants us to be willing to obey Him. But He calls the shots."

"Yeah, and my mom told me she wants to quit smoking and stuff, but she's going to need God's help to do it. In the meantime, I don't believe God's up there frowning down on her for it."

"So they wouldn't like kick her out of church for smoking?" asked Shonda with disbelief.

Beanie and I both laughed.

"Well, smoking inside the church building isn't allowed," I told her. "But she can smoke herself blue in the face out in the parking lot if she wants."

"And I've seen her do it too," said Beanie.

"And that's totally cool," I added. "I don't think anyone at church really judges her for it, and if they do, they shouldn't."

"The thing is," began Beanie, looking intently at both Shonda and Natala, "Jesus loves you just the way you are. He accepts you 'as is,' you know? He doesn't care what's going on in your life—I mean, it's not like He doesn't care. But He doesn't hold it against you if you've making mistakes and stuff. Sure, He expects you to start changing and growing and stuff once you give your life to Him.

But the Bible says that even when we didn't know Him and were just totally blowing it that Jesus still loved us anyway."

"Does that make any sense?" I asked them, since they both looked a little perplexed.

"Not really," admitted Shonda. "I always thought you had to act really good to be a Christian."

So we went over it again, this time focusing only on the part about Jesus loving them—unconditionally. And by the time we finished, I think they were getting it. But neither girl dropped onto her knees and prayed to be saved. Well, to be honest, I'm not sure what I would've done if they had. Although I feel confident that God would've led us. Still, I'm praying that our words will keep sinking in (and that they'll know God loves them). Also we invited them both to church tomorrow, but it didn't sound too likely that they'd come. Still you never know.

Sunday, May 12

Well, Shonda and Natala weren't at church today. I guess I'm not too surprised. As Grandma says, Rome wasn't built in a day. Duh. Talk about stating the obvious. But speaking of grandmas, Grandma O'Conner called me up from Pasadena today. I had e-mailed her about our cultural fair a while back, asking her if she or Grandpa had anything I could use for an Irish booth. So far, all I've come up with is a bunch of Saint Patrick's decorations that Mom told me I could use (from her school) as well as the possibility of baking loaves of Irish soda and brown bread (from recipes I found in one of Mom's old Irish cookbooks that used to belong to my dad's grandma). But I thought I'd start making and freezing loaves and then sell them for a few bucks each. (I plan to tie them with a green ribbon and a little paper shamrock.) Still, that doesn't seem quite enough for a whole booth.

So anyway Nana O'Conner called to tell me that she and Grandpa have gotten ahold of some Irish travel posters and stuff as well as some souvenirs that I could sell in the booth. She's sending a couple of big boxes this week. I asked her where she got the stuff (because I know they haven't been to Ireland lately—although they do go from time to time), and she told me that Grandpa has this friend over there who runs a tourist shop and he sold a bunch of stuff to Grandpa wholesale.

"Do I need to pay for it?" I asked, a little worried.

Nana just laughed. "Of course not. Just consider it our donation for your little Mexican orphans."

Well, I couldn't thank her enough. And believe me I've thanked God too because I know He had a hand in this! Especially since I'd been specifically praying that He'd show me what to do with my booth (since this event is only a couple weeks away now). My family's going to help me with the booth (although Benjamin refuses to dress up like a leprechaun!). And Mom said she'll donate the ingredients for the breads as well as help me bake them. So

I'm feeling pretty hopeful that it will be a success. Now I just hope (and pray) the other booths are all falling into place as well.

Tuesday, May 14 (poor Jewel)

Somehow with everything going on lately, I'd almost failed to realize that it's prom time again (not that I especially care since I'm obviously not going). But to be perfectly honest, I do feel kind of bad that I will be graduating from high school without ever having gone to the prom. I mean, both Beanie and Jenny and well, practically everyone else, it seems, has gone to the prom. But I'm trying not to think about that too much—or feel sorry for myself. And I'm believing that somehow God is going to make it up to me (since I'm trying to be obedient...). And if I start to feel sorry for myself, all I need to do is remember what it was like visiting Jewel at the hospital today. Because I'm sure she wishes she could go to the prom too.

I took Chloe with me, and although she was really quiet and seemed uncomfortable at first, she handled it pretty well. It's the second time I've actually seen Jewel in the hospital, but the first time was only briefly. (I waited outside her room while Anna visited for a few minutes yesterday.) But today was my first official "scheduled" visit (from seven to eight o'clock), and I have to admit it was really challenging. First of all, I'm not all that comfortable in hospitals (even when it was my best friend or my own mom I had a hard time, although I tried not to show it). But the truth is, I don't like the way hospitals smell or look or even sound. And I'm sure I could never be a nurse!

The way I feel isn't all that different from the way I reacted when I first saw the Mexican kids at the dump. It's like I don't want to touch anything or breathe the air or even be there. I know it's totally lame and slightly paranoid or phobic, (and I've never told anyone this) but to me, it's like the whole place is just crawling with germs and bacteria that I can't see. Still, I realize that Jesus told us to go visit the sick and the suffering, and so I'm learning to put these feelings aside. And I'm trying to trust God to protect me from germs (real or imagined).

Anyway, I'm not even sure if Jewel recognizes me. She mostly just lies there quietly (still with IV tubes and a shunt in her head and all that stuff that basically grosses me out), and she doesn't really react or do much of anything. But at least she's conscious and she seemed to look at both of us (with what seemed like interest). And so I just talked and talked to her. First I told her how I'd been praying for her and that I wanted her to know how much God loves her. I think I said a lot of the same things to her that Beanie and I had said to Natala and Shonda the other night (maybe that was good practice for me). I really felt pretty awkward and I kept wondering if she could understand anything I was saying at all. I just kept talking anyway. It's like I was afraid to allow a moment of silence (which I suppose is pretty silly), so I jabbered on and on like a battery-operated talking doll high on Energizers. At one point it seemed like she was almost smiling (or trying to). I think I might've been talking about the cultural fair about then (I'm not even sure), but somehow her face (or maybe it was God) encouraged me to reach over and take her hand (and remember I don't like touching things—or even people—in the hospital). But when I did she gave my hand a squeeze and I wondered if that was her way of saying she was glad I was there. And as silly as that may sound, it really touched me. Now I'm not really sure that's what it meant; she might have been trying to shut me up. But somehow it seemed important, like a message, and it made me want to go back to visit her again. I mean, even if it wasn't real easy, it was still good. And I think it was good for Chloe too. But on the way home, she admitted that seeing Jewel like that was really hard on her.

"I feel really bad for her," explained Chloe. "But it just looks so hopeless to me. Like I'm wondering wouldn't it be better if she had just died? I mean, who'd want to be stuck like that?"

"Obviously she wanted to die when she pulled the trigger, but I'm sure she must regret what she did by now. There's something about her that seems like she wants to be alive—even if it's like starting all over again. Couldn't you tell there was this little bit of spark in her?"

Chloe shrugged. "Maybe. But I really don't get it."

Then I asked her if she wanted to go back with me on Thursday (my next scheduled visit), and to my surprise she agreed. I thought for certain she'd turn me down.

Even as I write this, I really do understand what Chloe meant. (Although I didn't want to admit it to her, considering she still acts like suicide isn't such a big deal.) And to be perfectly honest, I don't know if I'd want to live under the circumstances that Jewel is facing. Anna said that it's not likely she'll ever develop beyond the mental state of a child now, and she'll probably always have some physical challenges to deal with. Still, with medical technology these days, you never know for sure. And I think we need to just hope for the best. Besides, I know of people who are mentally handicapped and live perfectly happy lives. Maybe Jewel can do that too. Especially with Jesus in her life. And despite how horrible her suicide attempt was, I really believe God has used it to touch a lot of people. So I guess good really can come out of evil.

DEAR GOD, PLEASE HELP JEWEL TO CONTINUE TO HEAL. I PRAY YOU'LL HEAL HER FROM THE INSIDE OUT. TOUCH HER HEART WITH YOUR LOVE AND YOUR FORGIVENESS. SHOW HER THAT YOU HAVE SOMETHING BETTER FOR HER. SOMETHING MORE. ENCOURAGE HER TO FIGHT TO RECOVER. AND, IF YOU'RE WILLING, PLEASE GOD, DO A MIRACLE! I BELIEVE YOU CAN MAKE HER WHOLE AGAIN. I ASK THAT YOU WOULD. AMEN.

SEVENTEEN

Wednesday, May 15 (talk about strange)

Jenny pulled me aside in the hallway this morning and told me we had to talk.

"I broke up with Trent last night," she whispered as she pulled me into a quiet corner. "And he's really upset."

I nodded, feeling slightly irked. "Yeah, well, what did you expect?"

"Well, he wanted me to go to the prom with him, and I just realized I couldn't. It wasn't fair. I mean, it's like he likes me so much, and I was feeling—well, like I could sort of take it or leave it. And it didn't seem fair for him to put all that money and energy into going to the prom with me feeling like that. Plus I'd feel so guilty I wouldn't want to break up with him right afterward, so I just decided to pull the plug and—"

"Yeah?" I interrupted her, glancing at my watch. "Hurry, Jenny, class is about to start."

"Okay, this is the thing, Cate. He's feeling so down, I

thought maybe you could be really nice to him—"

"Me?" I stared at her in confusion. "Why me?"

She sighed. "Oh, It's a long story. And you need to go to class."

I nodded. But then I noticed she was starting to cry. And I could barely remember the last time I'd seen Jenny cry. "What is it?" I asked, softening.

"Oh, nothing..." But now tears were streaming down her face.

"Jenny?"

She shook her head. "Go to class, Caitlin."

Well, now I felt stuck between that old proverbial rock and a hard place. I really should go to class, but one of my best friends was out in the hallway totally losing it. "Want to slip out for a cup of coffee?"

"Really?" Jenny eyed me with suspicion (she knows I am normally hugely opposed to skipping).

"Yeah, it's just history and I'm all caught up and everything." So we ducked out and zipped over to Starbucks, and Jenny told me what had happened.

"When I broke up with Trent he just started to totally fall apart. It was weird. I've never seen a guy act like that before. You know how Trent usually seems to have it all together and doesn't really show a lot of emotion. And anyway I just felt really bad for him—like a total creep. I mean, I had no idea that he cared that much for me. It was really kind of sweet."

I rolled my eyes. "Yeah, really sweet to break a guy's heart."

She frowned. "That's not what I mean."

"I know. I'm sorry. Go on."

"So anyway, I kept telling him I was sorry and that I never expected him to take it so hard. Finally I asked him if he was going to be okay." Jenny paused and looked around, almost as if to check and see if anyone else was listening. But the only other people in there were a couple in business clothes and totally uninterested in us. "And that's when he told me."

I waited. "What?"

She made a strange face, as if considering whether to tell me.

"What, Jenny?"

"You've got to promise not to tell."

I held up my hand as if to make a pledge. "I promise. Now what?"

"Trent thinks he may be gay."

"Gay?"

She nodded. "He told me that he'd been worried about his sexuality for some time now, and that's why he put the move on you last fall, and then when you rejected him, he put the move on me, thinking if I rejected him—it'd be like a sign or something. But he thought everything was cool when we were going out together. So did I. I mean, honestly, he never seemed gay to me. Of course, he never got real pushy about sex either." She paused to think.

"Oh, Jenny," I groaned, wondering where this conversation could possibly be headed.

"Anyway, I assumed the reason he wasn't pushing me was because I'd made it crystal clear we were not going to go there. In fact, I'm sure that's why our relationship lasted so long. The only reason I broke up with him was because I thought he was getting more serious than I wanted to be."

I sighed deeply, suddenly feeling way over my head. "But why are you telling me this, Jen?"

"Well, after I got home last night, I was worried that this whole thing might be my fault. You know, if I hadn't broken up with him everything would be fine. But it seems too late to fix that. And I got to thinking how Trent was interested in you before and—"

"What are you suggesting?"

"Well, I thought maybe you could seem interested in him—you know, to encourage him that he..."

"Isn't gay?"

She nodded sheepishly. "I know, it sounds kind of stupid now that I'm actually saying it out loud."

"Stupid? It sounds insane." I slowly shook my head in disbelief. "Do you honestly think it would make any difference?"

"I don't know. I just feel so bad, and well, sort of responsible."

I reached over and patted her arm. "I know it must be hard, but it's not your fault. And you've got to know that I can't do that, Jenny. First of all, it would be dishonest. But besides that, Trent's a smart guy; he'd see right through me—he knows I don't date. Then he might be hurt even more."

"Yeah. I can see that now. But I feel like I've got to do something."

"Can't you just be a friend to him?"

"I suggested that, but he got mad."

I thought for a moment. "Well, maybe I can be a friend to him."

"Would you, Caitlin? I'd appreciate it so much."

"I can try. But it's really up to Trent. And to be honest, I really don't know a whole lot about homosexuality. I mean, in psychology we learned that people are born that way. But I also know that the Bible says it's wrong. I've never really given it much thought, but it seems kind of confusing."

"Yeah, I don't really know what to think either. I mean I really like Trent a lot. He's such a cool guy. And I don't think I would think any less of him if he really was gay. But to be honest, I hope he's not."

"I wonder what makes him think he's gay?"

"Yeah, me too. I mean, here we are going out together and he's not acting gay. Then I break up and he says that. I mean, to be perfectly honest, it doesn't make me look too good." Jenny laughed nervously.

I smiled. "So is that what worries you?"

"No, silly. But how would you feel?"

I shrugged. "See, these are some of the problems I avoid by not dating."

"Please, Caitlin, don't start getting smug with me. I'm already having a bad day. I don't need any sermons right now."

"Okay, I'll control myself." Then I noticed the clock on the wall and suggested we'd better get back.

At lunchtime I looked for Trent and finally spotted him sitting off by himself at a corner table. I went over and asked if I could join him.

"Is this a mission of mercy?" he asked dryly.

"Maybe." I sat down. "I heard Jen broke up with you and thought maybe you could use a friend."

He eyed me curiously. "How much did she tell you?"

I took a bite of my salad and avoided his gaze, wondering how to answer.

"Oh, man!" he said as he shoved his tray aside. "I'll bet the whole school knows."

"Trent," I said quietly. "Just chill. The only reason Jenny told me is because she really likes you and cares about you. She's really upset and feels kind of responsible."

He laughed sarcastically. "Yeah, she probably thinks she broke my heart and sent me running to the other side. Yeah, you bet!"

Now I studied him carefully. "Well, then maybe you need to do some explaining, Trent. I mean, here you two were going out—you were a couple—and now... Well, think about it, it's kind of shocking."

"It's nobody's business." His voice was hard.

"Maybe not. But when you told Jenny, you involved her; you made it her business."

"Yeah, and she told you and now it's your business. And then you probably told Beanie and it's her business and she told—"

"I didn't tell anyone. Come on, Trent, you can trust me."

He looked at me and sighed. "Yeah, maybe I can. But still, my sexuality is none of your business."

"I agree, totally. And the only reason I came over was because I thought you could use a friend."

His face softened just slightly. "Yeah, I suppose it could be lonely to come out of the closet in a place like this."

I tried to ignore that. "And we used to be pretty good friends, last fall, do you remember?"

He nodded. "Yeah, I even thought I had a crush on you for a while."

I smiled. "And to be honest, I had just a little bit of a crush on you too."

He rolled his eyes. "Yeah, I bet you're just saying that—hoping you can dissuade me from the boys."

"Oh, Trent!" I made a face. "Honestly! Don't you remember that night when I told you all about my non-dating thing? The only reason I told you was because I was afraid I might compromise it for you."

"Really?" His eyes brightened just a little.

"And then it wasn't long before you and Jen got together. At first I was even a little jealous, but then I was okay."

Then he grew quiet and I paused to munch on my turkey sandwich for a bit, praying silently as I ate that I would come up with something helpful to say, something that might really make a difference, but my mind was pretty much blank. Finally I pushed my tray away and said what I felt. "You know, Trent, I just don't get it."

"What do you mean?"

"You know. How can you know you're gay?"

He shrugged. "I can't really explain it."

"But didn't you uh—have—feelings for Jenny?"

"I guess so, maybe."

"Then what in the world would make you think you're gay all of a sudden?"

That's when his face turned totally hard, and I sensed our conversation was about to end. "Look, Caitlin, I appreciate your friendship. But this isn't psychology class, you know. And I really don't need you trying to fix me with all your Christianity crud either. My sexuality is a private issue and I'd prefer to keep it that way."

"I'm sorry." I forced a stiff smile. "Can we still be friends?" I asked meekly.

His stony face broke (just a little). "Okay, but just don't push it."

"All right. But can I ask you one more question, Trent?"

His eyes narrowed. "Can I really stop you?"

I didn't flinch. "Not without making a scene."

He sighed. "Go ahead then."

"Do you have someone you can talk to about this stuff?"

Now he laughed—only it was a really harsh laugh. "Oh yeah, sure."

"I mean someone good, someone you can trust?"

"Just who can you trust, Caitlin? Your Jesus?" He stood

now. "You think your Jesus can fix everything? You think He can even fix me?"

Before I could answer he walked away, and I felt like I'd been slapped. But somehow (after the sting went away) I realized that Trent hadn't really meant to hurt me (at least I don't think he did). And I prayed for him off and on throughout the day. I didn't tell Jenny much about our conversation but encouraged her to keep praying for him. I told her that I think he's really hurting inside, deeply, and although I don't really know why, I think he's trying to deal with it. Or maybe God is. But somehow I think things are going to be changing for him.

With all this still on my mind, I went to midweek church tonight and afterward I talked with Tony, and (under the confidentiality code of the pulpit) I told him about Trent and how worried I was for him. I think in light of what happened with Jewel I might be a little overly sensitive, but something about Trent's hopelessness sent a chill down my spine today. And I would feel so horrible if he tried something like what Jewel did—and what if he succeeded?

Anyway Tony told me I was right to be concerned and that he'd be glad to talk to Trent anytime. He also said that suicide is the third cause of death among teens (news to me!) and something he always took very seriously. But then he told me something that really blew my mind.

"I think I might know what Trent is struggling with, Caitlin." He spoke quietly, and I could tell this wasn't something he wanted to announce to the whole congregation, although by then there were only a few stragglers left. "Steph knows all about this, and I tell people when I feel it's appropriate, but I had some similar problems when I was a kid."

"You mean you thought you were gay?" I said quietly.

"Well, let's just say someone tried to plant that idea in my head."

"Really?"

He nodded. "I was only in junior high at the time, and it was someone I really respected, too. Plus that was the era when everyone was coming out of the closet, and people were starting to act like it was cool to be gay."

"So what happened?"

"Well, I finally went to my pastor in desperation. I told him what was going on. And fortunately for me, he was a good man, and not only did he graciously straighten me out on a few things, but he took that other person to task as well. Still, the whole thing was pretty hard on me. And if not for God and my pastor, I honestly don't know where I'd be today."

"Man, Tony, I can't believe you just told me all that. Thanks."

He smiled. "Like I said, it's not something I tell everyone. But because of your friendship with Trent, I felt I should. And anyway, I've been amazed at how many times God has used that whole episode to help someone else. I can honestly say I'm thankful for having gone through it. You know, God really is the Blessed Redeemer, Caitlin."

"Yeah, I'm seeing that more and more."

"If you're comfortable telling Trent that I'd like to talk to him, I wouldn't mind a bit if you share some of my story with him—especially if it would encourage him to come for counsel."

"Thanks, Tony. It might help. I mean, he seems pretty skeptical about God and church right now. You know he considers himself an atheist. But at the same time, he seems pretty hopeless too. I think he could use a really good counselor."

Tony handed me his business card. "Tell him to call me anytime. And if it'll make him feel better, Steph is always more than willing to attend the counseling sessions."

"Steph?"

"Well, in this situation it can be helpful to have a woman around."

"Oh." I nodded. "Okay."

And so tomorrow, I hope to give Tony's card to Trent. I mean, what can it hurt? In the meantime I'll be praying.

DEAR GOD, PLEASE HELP ME TO BREAK THROUGH TO TRENT. HELP HIM TO KNOW THAT YOU'RE NOT WHO HE THINKS YOU ARE. AND HELP HIM TO BE WILLING TO TALK TO TONY. I CONFESS THAT I REALLY DON'T UNDERSTAND THIS WHOLE GAY THING, BUT I KNOW YOU DO. AND I ALSO KNOW THAT TRENT SEEMS TOTALLY MISERABLE RIGHT NOW. I KNOW YOU HAVE BETTER THINGS FOR HIM. PLEASE HELP HIM TO FIND YOU IN A REAL AND LASTING WAY. AMEN.

EIGHTEEN

Friday, May 17 (feeling hopeful...)

Well, I gave Trent Tony's card yesterday and he acted like "Forget it." But I tried not to seem offended and just encouraged him to give it a try. And although I'm not sure he was listening, I did tell him a little about Tony. But mostly Trent acted like he couldn't care less. And he seemed even more depressed than the day before. But today he told me that he'd called and made an appointment for tomorrow morning. I tried to act cool (not get all excited) and told him I didn't think he'd be sorry. So now I'm just really praying that Tony will get through to him. Not so much about the gay thing—because honestly I'm not sure what's up with that—but that Tony gets through to him about God. If anyone can reach Trent, I'd put my money on Tony.

Last night, Chloe and I went to see Jewel again. And to our amazement, she said "hi" and a couple of other words that her therapist must've taught her this week.

Mrs. Garcia was there when we arrived, and she just looked so totally worn out. I know this whole ordeal must be really hard on her. She told me that she had to pick up her boys from the baby-sitter and take them over to her mom's since she had to work the night shift to make extra money since they don't have any insurance. And it was all I could do not to just spill the beans about our cultural fair and how half the proceeds would be going to her family. (We voted to keep it quiet until after the fair, when we could hand them the check—just in case anything goes wrong.) So I told her that we're all still praying for her and Jewel and wanted to do anything we could to help out.

"Just knowing you kids are coming over here like this to visit my baby is the best help I can get right now." She turned and looked back at her daughter, rolling one of Jewel's dark curls around her finger. "She said 'Mama' today." And I could see her eyes getting wet.

"I'm praying that she'll get completely well," I told her, trying to appear more confident than I actually felt just then. Somehow seeing Jewel in the hospital like that sort of saps my faith.

"Me too," she said as she clutched her shiny red purse to her. "And I know the good Lord has my baby in His hands."

"So you're a Christian?" I don't know why this surprised me. Maybe because Jewel had been such a wild child before all this happened (but then I should know better than to judge parents by their kids or vice versa).

"Oh yes, I don't know if I could've survived what life's dished out if not for my Lord and Savior. But it's true I haven't been to church in years. I usually have to work on Sundays. But I've never stopped believing—and I stop and light a candle for her whenever I can. Then I sit here by Jewel and read from the Good Book every single day."

So go figure. Jewel's mom's a believer. For some reason that encouraged me a lot. And later, when I sat down to talk with Jewel I even mentioned this. And it might've been my imagination, but I think I saw her eyes light up when I said the name of Jesus. And I really think something's going on inside her right now.

But what was really incredible was how Chloe actually spoke to Jewel last night. First she asked her how she was doing and then told her what the weather was like outside, and then to my total amazement, Chloe sang her a song. And Chloe has an absolutely beautiful voice. Kind of low and throaty—not like you'd expect from a fourteen-year-old girl. And Jewel really seemed to like it. I could see her fingers tapping on the blanket, like she was trying to keep time, although she was just a little off beat.

On the way home I asked Chloe about the song she'd sung (I'd never heard it before), and she told me she'd made it up!

"You're kidding?"

"No, I make up songs all the time. Usually I play them with my guitar."

"Wow, you should think about doing that professionally."

She just shrugged. "Oh, it's nothing, really."

"No, Chloe, it's not nothing. You're really gifted. Has anyone ever heard you sing?"

She shrugged again. "Not really. It's usually something I just do on my own to alleviate boredom. I hadn't planned to sing tonight; it just sort of happened."

"I think Jewel really liked it."

Chloe smiled. And I realized how little I'd seen her smile.

"Maybe you could bring your guitar next time," I suggested. "I mean, if you want to come again, that is. I know it's not all that easy."

"Yeah, after the last time I wondered why in the world I'd agreed to come again. But now I'm thinking I kind of like it. I mean, I think it's making me appreciate that I'm alive or something. Plus I like it that Jewel can't really respond—not that I don't want her to. But it's kind of freeing being around her. In fact, I'm wondering if it'd be okay for me to just visit her on my own sometimes."

"I'm sure it would. I'll give you Anna's phone number. She's the one who handles the schedule. I know there are still lots of times when no one's there. And I think it must be pretty sad for Jewel to be all on her own like that."

"Yeah, it must be really lonely."

When I dropped her at her house, I told her again that I really meant what I said about her singing. "You're really good, Chloe. You should know that. Really, I was totally blown away by your voice."

I noticed a little pink glow in her cheeks, sweet and innocent and an odd contrast to her spiky hair and piercings. "Thanks, Caitlin. I appreciate it. And thanks for taking time to spend with me. I know it must be pretty boring hanging with a junior high kid."

"Chloe, I don't even think about your age anymore. I mean, you're really smart and you're pretty mature for your age." I laughed. "Not like my little brother who can really act like a goofball sometimes. I can't believe he'll actually be in eighth grade next year. But then I've heard that boys don't mature as soon as girls."

"Oh, I think Ben is sweet."

I eyed her curiously. "But probably not your type, huh?"

She shook her head. "No, but he's a nice kid."

Saturday, May 18 (hilarious idea)

This afternoon Beanie and Jenny and I went to the mall together (first time we've all three done that in ages). And it was just like old times. We were silly and goofy and even went looking at prom dresses (pretending that we were actually going to the prom).

"Hey, why don't we?" said Jenny suddenly.

I just rolled my eyes. "Oh, sure, you mean like the Sadie Hawkins dance—just go out and invite some guys for a one-night thing? Or maybe we should hire some sort of male escort service."

"No, Caitlin, I mean maybe the three of us could go together!"

Beanie started giggling. "Oh yeah, sure. I s'pose you think you can get me to wear a tux."

"No, we'll all wear prom dresses and just go as a girls trio. We can even go out there and dance if we want to. Or we can just hang out and watch people."

"Jenny, you're nuts!"

"Why? Are you afraid?"

I stood up straight. "No. But I know you can't be serious."

"I'm totally serious. I wouldn't want to do it with just two girls—they might think we were gay or something. But I think we could get away with doing it with three girls. I would think you'd love this idea, Cate. I mean, it could be like really making a statement about not dating."

"And you were just whining about how you were the only one who hasn't been to a prom," Beanie reminded me.

"I told you not to repeat that," I told her.

"I'm not afraid to do it," said Beanie. "I think it'd be a hoot."

"Are you in, Caitlin?" asked Jenny.

And so I agreed. And as crazy it sounded, I started thinking it might be fun. At least until we started looking at the price tags of the dresses and considered the cost of prom tickets and everything.

"I'm trying to save my money," I admitted.

Beanie sighed. "Me too."

"Yeah, it does seem a little silly to put out that much

money for just one night. But how about if we go retro?"

"I can get into that," said Beanie eagerly. "And I know just the places to look."

And so it was we hit all the thrift shops in town as well as Jenny's attic. And we finally came up with three very retro outfits that actually looked pretty cool. Okay, I'll admit that at first I thought we looked a little like hookers or disco dancers or something from an Archie comic book, but then didn't everyone in the seventies look like that? My dress is a little sequined affair with bright psychedelic stripes of aqua blue, lime green, and hot pink. I'll wear it with knee-high boots (very white and shiny) and several strings of beads. We all plan to wear white or really pale lipstick and lots of gaudy eye shadow and fake eyelashes. It should be pretty funny. I showed my parents my outfit and they both just totally cracked up.

"It's like a bad sixties flashback," said my dad, pretending to squint.

"I kind of like it," my mom confessed. "I remember seeing teenagers dressed like that when I was just a little kid, and I wanted to dress like them, but I wasn't old enough."

"Maybe I should hang on to it in case you want to wear it sometime," I teased my mom.

"Hey, that's not a bad idea, but I'd have to lose a few pounds to fit into that tiny thing. But who knows, maybe by next Halloween."

Then I carefully removed my outfit (since it already needs a seam mended) and went down to help Mom make a couple batches of soda bread. And it was fun being with her in the kitchen. She seems pretty much back to normal now (after losing her baby). And it's good to hear her laugh again. I'm afraid to bring it up, but I do wonder how she feels about the whole thing now. I mean, is she kind of relieved not to be pregnant and about to undergo a real life-changing event? Or does she still wish she were having a baby? Maybe I'll never know for certain.

Monday, May 20 (the boxes came!)
Wow! Nana and Grandpa really came through with the Irish stuff. I got two boxes packed full of all sorts of Irish trinkets (linen towels, small pieces of pottery, inexpensive jewelry, T-shirts...) as well as some nice big posters. My booth is going to look totally great. And every night this week, Mom and I will be making either soda bread or brown bread. Dad says he's already put on five pounds just smelling it baking. And Ben's been really helpful cutting shamrocks out of green construction paper (to be stapled all over the booth). It feels almost like Christmas at our house (well, make that an Irish Christmas).

What's kind of cool about this is that it's got Dad remembering things his grandpa (the one who originally immigrated from Ireland around the turn of the century) told him as a little boy. And so while we're making bread and stuff, Dad sits there on the counter stool and (using a pretty bad Irish brogue) tells us stories about "the old country." And I never realized those poor Irish people had it so hard. It's like getting a free (and somewhat humorous) history lesson in our very own kitchen.

"Someone should write these stories down," I told my dad as I filled another bread pan with dough.

"Well, you're the writer, lassie," he said. "I'll be leavin' that all up to you now."

"Oh, sure, make me the family historian," I pretended to complain. "I mean, it's not like I don't already have enough to do."

"But you are a good writer, honey," said my mom. "Which reminds me—are you thinking about your major yet?"

I groaned. "Please, don't remind me about that. Besides, I don't have to figure that out right away."

"I know, but I just hope you won't forget what a good writer you are. You know, it's wrong to waste talent, Caitlin."

"Yeah, but anyone can write. It's no big deal." Suddenly my words reminded me of Chloe and how easily she'd dismissed her musical abilities. "But I'll think about it," I quickly added, not wanting to endure any more lecturing on the subject. Then I suddenly remembered how the language arts director (Mr. Olinski) had asked me to submit a thousand-word essay for the state writing contest last spring. I haven't even told anyone else about it, because I'm so certain I don't have a chance. I mean, I don't even write very good essays in the first place. Plus I know the one I did must be pretty lame (although it was about the Mexican kids). But the problem was I wrote it too fast because so much was going on just then, and I handed it in too late to get any editing help or critiquing on it. I probably shouldn't have even wasted the school's money to submit it (Mr. Olinski told me there was an application fee). But hopefully he's forgotten all about it by now. I know I did.

Saturday, May 25 (the big day!)

Man, am I ever exhausted! But, oh, was it worth it! The cultural fair was a total success. I think almost everyone in town must've come. And to think I'd been worried (after setting up my booth) that we had too much stuff to possibly sell all of it. But we sold every single thing! Our booth alone made over seven hundred dollars!!! It was totally amazing.

I couldn't believe how great all the other booths were too. Everyone just really came through with flying colors. It was incredible. Even the mayor stopped by to congratulate me, and a photographer from the paper took my picture (along with a bunch of others, but I might be in tomorrow's paper). Steph is acting as treasurer, and we won't know the total until tomorrow. But I suspect it's a lot. I can't wait to hear. The fair ended at six, and then it took us a couple hours to tear down. But Martha got several local pizza places to donate pizzas to the workers, so we took a nice break and stuffed ourselves. Trent was even there (actually helping Jenny with the Scandinavian booth), and the two seemed to be acting

like old friends. Jenny told me that he's had several sessions with Tony, and while she couldn't give me any
details (for which I'm grateful), she thinks it's going really
well.

The African-American booth (the biggest one of all
the booths) was a big hit with all kinds of great foods—
everything from black-eyed peas to great big chunks of
the best corn bread I've ever tasted. And both Shonda
and Natala worked in it all day.

There's just too much to even begin to write about,
but the bottom line is "All God's Children" hit a home run
today. And it looks like it'll be back again next year.
Although I'm thankful to say I probably won't be quite as
involved. I mean, I'd like to do something, but I'm ready to
let someone else jump in and help out. And now I'm totally
exhausted and plan to thank God for this fantastic and
amazing day and then crash. I might even sleep until
Monday!

NINETEEN

Sunday, May 26 (ahhh...)

Well, I didn't sleep until Monday after all.
Actually, I wanted to hear the financial outcome of yesterday's fair and knew I'd have to get my tired, aching
body off to church if I wanted to get the news firsthand. And it was good news.

"All God's Children" made $15,843.25! Wowsers! That
sounds like a small fortune to me. I know even half of
that will do a whole lot for the garbage dump kids. But
here's what really blew me away today. When Pastor
Tony made the big announcement, he also said that the
church had decided to finance my trip down there this
summer to present the funds! I was so happy I stood up
and cried in front of the entire congregation. I felt
pretty stupid but totally happy too. I mean, I'd already
saved up enough to get me down there and back
(whether anyone from church goes or not). My parents still

aren't too thrilled with the idea of me going down there alone, but the mission has assured me that they will arrange to have someone come up and escort me from the border so I really don't think there's anything to wig out over.

I couldn't wait to e-mail Josh the news. Okay, it probably sounds like I'm bragging now, but our fund-raiser actually did better than his. Although, to be perfectly fair, his raised more money for Mexico than ours since 100 percent of their funds will go down there instead of half. Still, I'm not sorry that the Garcia family is getting half. We have a committee that will meet Jewel's mom at the hospital tomorrow to give her the check. (Joel's in charge of this one.) And even though our gift won't even begin to cover the hospital expenses, I think it will be encouraging, and I hope it will make a difference.

All in all, the cultural fair was a great experience and I learned a lot. Still, I can't pretend that I'm not happy (and hugely relieved) that it is over now. And I'm looking forward to just hanging with my friends and living a more "normal" life (whatever that is?). Next week is the prom, and we haven't told anyone what we're doing. I didn't even tell Anna (when she was feeling sorry that I wouldn't be there). She's so happy to be going with Joel—thankfully they're still together, although I wonder how long it will last. (And almost hope I'm not around when it ends—isn't that terrible of me?)

Wednesday, May 29 (job switch?)

First I want to say that it was totally and unbelievably cool when Joel presented Jewel's mom with that check. She just broke down and cried. She couldn't even talk. And pretty soon most of us were crying too. But finally she said thank you (over and over) and then we all started hugging. I don't know if everyone felt as jazzed as I did, but I have a feeling they did. And now I totally believe that it really is better to give than to receive because I can't imagine anyone giving me anything that could make me any happier than how I felt when I saw how touched Jewel's mom was by our gift.

THANK YOU, GOD!

But now here's the latest news flash in the constantly changing life of Caitlin Renee O'Conner. Beanie found out on Monday that she'd been hired by the park district to work at the day care center at the park all summer. And she was sooo glad. First, because it gets her out of the Pizza Hut, plus she only works weekdays, and on top of that she'll get paid more. She was going on and on about it, when stupid, stupid me! What was I thinking? Obviously I wasn't! Anyway, I made this totally lame wisecrack about how it wasn't fair to get paid as much as I make for just playing with rug rats and curtain climbers all day (like my job is so mentally challenging—not!). But as I mentioned, I just wasn't thinking (or maybe I was...). And naturally she took offense. Not seriously, thank goodness, but enough to ignite a lively debate. (And of course it happened in the lunchroom, so lots of kids were listening).

"Well, you know, for someone who acts like she really loves kids, I'd think you'd want a job just like mine."

I suppose it was the way she said the word acts (like I've just been pretending to be committed to these kids all along) that made me start being a little smug. "No, that's okay. I mean, I wouldn't want to give up my cushy office job where I just sit in a comfy chair all day with air-conditioning and a Starbucks right next door."

"Yeah, that's what I figured," she said. "You're getting soft, Caitlin."

I laughed. "Hey, what am I supposed to do? Run down to Parks and Recreation and see if I can steal your job?"

Suddenly her eyes lit up. "Nooo," she said slowly, and it looked as if those mischievous wheels were turning round in her head. "But maybe if you're really serious about those Mexican kids and you really want to get some good experience with kids—then just maybe you and I shouldn't see if we could switch jobs."

"Switch jobs?" I eyed her curiously. "What are you saying, Beanie?"

"Well, I've had enough business classes to do your job, and you've had as much experience as me to get my job. Maybe we should go talk to our bosses and see if we can just switch."

"Beanie," I began, "excuse me for saying so, but that sounds totally nuts!"

She pointed her finger at me. "Oh, really? Well, maybe it's just because you're not really willing to spend time with kids. I mean, you talk like you want to spend the rest of your life working with poor orphans, but are you really willing to roll up your pretty little sleeves and get some real hands-on experience in the trenches?"

Now, it didn't help matters that several kids at our table actually cheered when she said this. But as I've said before, Beanie is gifted in the dramatic department. And this audience was playing right into her hands.

"It just sounds so impossible," I said weakly.

"Nothing's impossible with God." She smiled smugly.

But suddenly, her words seemed to kick in. I hated to admit it, especially in front of all my peers, but I suspected Beanie was right on. "You know, you might be onto something. But really, I don't know about a job switch. I mean, we'd both have to do interviews and—"

"So are you willing to give it a try then?"

"Maybe. But I'd still like to think about it a little."

And so I did think about it. And I prayed about it. And today at work I told Rita about the whole crazy idea and she seemed to think it made sense too.

"As much as I'd hate to lose you, I think your friend might be right. If you're really serious about working with underprivileged kids, then I'd think you'd want some opportunities to get some real-life experience first."

"But do you think Beanie would have a very good chance at getting my job?"

"As good as anyone. And maybe even better if you recommend her."

And so it's settled. Beanie and I are going to give this crazy idea a shot. She still has to talk to the day care people. But we figure we've got nothing to lose (except my pride...). Because first of all, I might not get the job, and then I have to admit that the idea of working with little kids all summer has got me feeling fairly nervous. I mean, what if Beanie is right? What if I AM all talk? And what if I end up looking like an absolute fool? Still, I'll never know if I don't give this thing a try. And so I'm actually praying that God will open the door and let me see what I'm made of.... Gulp.

DEAR GOD, EVERY TIME I TURN AROUND I FEEL LIKE I'M GETTING BOMBARDED WITH A NEW SIDE OF MYSELF (AND SOMETIMES I DON'T LIKE WHAT I SEE OR WHERE IT SEEMS I'M GOING). BUT I BELIEVE YOU'RE AT WORK IN MY LIFE. AND ONCE AGAIN I WANT TO TOTALLY ENTRUST YOU WITH THE OUTCOME. IF IT'S THE RIGHT THING FOR ME TO WORK AT THE DAY CARE CENTER, I PRAY YOU'LL JUST KICK OPEN THAT DOOR. AND IF NOT, I'LL BE HAPPY TO STAY WHERE I AM. I JUST WANT YOUR WILL, GOD. AMEN.

Friday, May 31 (here goes nothing)
Well, believe it or not, we're trying. I went in to interview

for Beanie's job and she interviewed for mine. We won't know the results until Monday, but we're both feeling fairly positive. (Actually I think she's feeling more positive than I am.) But surprisingly when the woman who interviewed me heard why we were doing this, she was really nice and supportive (she didn't even treat me or Beanie like total nutcases!). And the really surprising thing was how much I liked it at the day care center. I mean, I just felt right at home. I even stayed a while and played with the kids after nap time. And suddenly I'm really hoping (and praying hard) that this thing happens. Pretty weird, huh? One day you think you're going to be doing one thing all summer and the next day everything just changes. But I think I'm starting to handle changes better. I mean, I used to really get uptight when things started changing. I guess by nature I'm kind of a control freak. But I really don't want to be. I'd like to be more free and loose (trusting God to take care of things). And while I'm sure I've come a long way, I know I have a long, long way to go.

But the possibility of doing this job switch with Beanie gave me another idea. Suddenly I'm thinking maybe I should invite Beanie to come to Mexico with me. I mean, I had already saved up enough money and now the church has decided to send me.... And I know having Beanie along would probably make my parents feel better. Plus she really got into helping those kids last summer. So, anyway, I'm going to pray about it. And I'll ask my parents (and maybe Tony and Steph) and see what they think. But I'm thinking it could be pretty cool for the two of us to go down there together for a week (or maybe two!).

Well, tomorrow's the big night (prom!). Tee-hee. To be perfectly honest, I feel kind of like a prom crasher, but the three of us bought our tickets so it's not like we're sneaking in or anything—it's totally legit. And we decided if we don't have fun or someone gives us a bad time, then we'll just hightail it outta there and go see a movie or something. We haven't told anyone at school what we're up to, but it was hard not to snicker today when others were talking about the prom and looking at us with pity in their eyes.

I did tell Josh (via e-mail) about our intended caper. And he wrote back saying that he wished he could see us and to make sure we get a photo and scan it so I can send it to him. It's funny; now that I know we're going to be at different colleges next year, I'm feeling really comfortable chatting with him via e-mail. For a little while I was getting kind of uptight, like I didn't want to seem too friendly (like I was coming on to him), which I know is silly, but it's true. And now I'm feeling all relaxed and easy— it's like we've better friends now than ever.

And he's so appreciative of the time I'm spending with Chloe. Apparently he called her last week, and she told him about visiting Jewel and how I've been encouraging her to take her music seriously and how she likes spending time with me. That meant a lot to me since it's sometimes hard to read that girl. I mean, I really like and admire her and she seems way older than fourteen sometimes. But she's so protective of her feelings and stuff that I sometimes wonder if she just wishes she could blow me off. But maybe not.

Sunday, June 2 (what a hoot!)

Well, we three chicks caused quite a sensation at the prom last night (and ended up staying for pretty much the whole thing). But here's an unexpected twist. Last night before we left, Trent called Jenny and they had a long heart-to-heart. And then Jenny called me and Beanie and asked if we could invite Trent to join us as our escort. She said he was feeling better about things but pretty blue that he was going to miss out on the prom. Beanie and I agreed after making Jenny promise that there was absolutely nothing romantic going on between the two of them. It's one thing to have Trent escort the three of us, but something altogether different if they think it's a double date (Trent and Jenny, and me and Beanie!). But Trent was totally diplomatic and traded off dances equally between the three of us (if anything he neglected Jenny).

Then a couple times we all four went out and danced together holding hands. Trent had on this really great tangerine orange tux that he and Beanie had somehow unearthed today. It was straight out of the seventies with bell-bottoms and big ruffles on the shirt and shiny white platform shoes! Too much.

The whole evening was just crazy and fun (and we got lots of photos!). We even got nominated as the "Three-Headed Prom Queen and King Lucky Strike." (I think someone was trying to undermine Jessica Taylor, or Miss Snooty Pants, as Beanie used to call her in junior high.) But as it turned out Jessica and her latest beau (Carl Fitzgerald) won. (Although there were accusations that Jessica had paid friends to stuff the ballot box.)

The totally cool thing was how Anna and Joel came in second (prince and princess). And I have never seen Anna look so completely jazzed (not to mention gorgeous!). We'd all voted for them and then cheered loudly when their names were announced. It was like a real Cinderella story, and I was totally thrilled for Anna. Still, at the same time, I couldn't help but think about Jewel (stuck in her hospital bed and trying to learn how to eat with a spoon again). I don't think anyone was surprised not to see Jamal at the prom (although Natala had invited him to be her date). But I heard rumors that he was spending the evening with Jewel at the hospital. I hope it's true.

Toward the end of the evening, Trent had invited me onto the floor for a slow dance, and while we were dancing he thanked me for recommending Tony to him.

"He's a pretty cool guy," Trent admitted.

"Yeah, I couldn't believe how lucky I got when my aunt married him and I got to have him for my uncle."

"Well, I just wanted you to know that he's really helping me to sort through everything."

"That's cool."

"Yeah, I was pretty confused. But it's starting to feel like the fog's lifting."

I leaned back and looked into Trent's face. "I'm really glad for you. I hated seeing you so miserable."

"Well, as much as I hated it when Jenny broke up with me, sometimes it's good to work through these things; like you come out stronger in the end."

I nodded. "Yeah, I suppose you're right."

And so now I'm sitting here thinking about how Trent is probably right. I mean, I suppose if I had my way I'd like to help everyone just avoid all kinds of pain related to dating—by eliminating it completely. But then these things aren't really up to me (as my friends have made totally clear on more than one occasion). And anyway, I'm thinking about how Beanie got involved with Joel. And as a result of their friendship, Joel came to church with her, became a Christian, and now seems to be doing really great. And then Jenny was dating Trent and even though it nearly destroyed him when she broke up with him, he's now looking for help in all the right places. Oh, sure, he still claims to be an atheist and all, but like Jenny says, she was too just a year ago. And I am not giving up on Trent! So, go figure, Caitlin O'Conner! Of course, I am NOT saying that dating is a good way to get guys to come to church. But I guess it's not my place to tell others what to do either. And besides, I've seen firsthand how God really can work in amazing ways.

DEAR GOD, YOU ARE SO TOTALLY AMAZING! I MEAN, EVERY SINGLE TIME I THINK I HAVE YOU ALMOST FIGURED OUT, YOU GO AND SURPRISE ME BIG TIME! I JUST PRAY THAT YOU'LL HELP ME TO ALWAYS KEEP MY EYES AND EARS WIDE OPEN AND THAT I'LL NEVER, EVER TRY TO PUT YOU IN A BOX. I'M GLAD YOU'RE SO MUCH BIGGER AND GREATER THAN I CAN IMAGINE. AND I THANK YOU FOR ALL YOU'RE DOING IN ME AND THE PEOPLE AROUND ME. I CAN REALLY SEE HOW YOU'RE ANSWERING THE JABEZ PRAYER IN MY LIFE. I LOVE YOU!!! AMEN.

TWENTY

Well, it's official. I'll be working with the rug rats and Beanie will be answering phones. And while I know Beanie thinks she's getting the best end of the deal, I am totally excited about this switcheroo. And today Rita suggested that I start training Beanie tomorrow. That way she and I can share shifts this week (allowing us both some extra time off right before graduation). Plus this is senior skip week so we have a little extra time anyway. How great to just hang out or sleep in or whatever. Pretty nice.

Beanie and I went out for burritos tonight to celebrate our job situation, and I decided to ask her about Mexico (after getting encouragement from both Tony and my parents). At first she was a little worried about missing out on work (and she hasn't even started yet!), but then she stopped herself.

"I guess if I'm really trusting God, I should trust that

He'll take care of everything whether I miss a week of work or not. Right?"

I nodded. "Makes sense to me. Let's not forget how God wants to bless us with what we need. And just the way He's provided for Mexico is a huge encouragement for me."

"But are you sure you want to use your travel money for me?"

"Oh, Beanie, I would so totally love it if you could come."

"I'd really like to."

"Then just say yes."

"How about if I pray about it?"

"Great."

After that we stopped by to visit Jewel. Anna said that her visitors have really dwindled lately—probably with graduation so near—plus it's not that easy to go and spend time with her. Believe me, I know. It seems like her progress is so slow. And yet she's actually saying short sentences now. And she remembers our names when we come. So that's something. But perhaps the best part is how much she likes to talk about and hear about Jesus. I mean, she's just like a little kid the way her eyes light up whenever she hears that name.

I suppose in some ways it's even challenging to us to be more like her—in that sweet, childlike way. It's like she's just totally in love with Jesus. And if you'd known Jewel before the accident and then saw her now, you would never believe it was the same person. It almost seems like, although her physical and mental body have been handicapped, her spirit has been completely released. It doesn't quite make sense, but it's pretty cool to see.

Still, I don't think most of her friends quite get that. I know that Shonda and Natala have become increasingly more uncomfortable with each visit. Shonda confessed to me last week that she feels really guilty for not going over there more, but that she gets so depressed afterward that it doesn't seem worth it. And I don't quite get that because I don't ever feel depressed after visiting. In fact, it's almost the opposite. But to be honest, I still have a hard time going at first, it's like I have to climb over this big obstacle, kind of like a roadblock. But once that's done I'm okay. Beanie said she feels the same way.

Before we left today, we sang "Jesus Loves Me" several times and Jewel got most of the words right by the last time. Her mom says it's her favorite song now (quite a change from the old rap music she used to love). So while it's hard to see her not progressing faster, she still seems pretty happy. And I'm still praying for a miracle—for a complete recovery.

Tuesday, June 4 (Beanie's first day)

Beanie did a great job today. I told her that she's learning a lot faster than I did, and I think it made her feel good (since she had plenty of mishaps too). But I remember how frustrated I was during my first week, and I want her transition to be smoother (partly to convince Rita that I wasn't wrong in giving such a strong recommendation).

But when Anna came down (to ride home), her face looked sad.

"What's wrong?" I asked.

"It's Jewel. Her mom just called and asked that we pray. I guess Jewel's got some sort of infection and swelling going on inside her head."

"We just saw her yesterday and she seemed fine," said Beanie.

"Well, according to her mom, she's not fine now."

"Do you think we should stop by and visit?" I asked.

"No, her mom says they want to keep her as quiet as possible for now."

So as we drove home we took turns praying for Jewel. And by the time I'd dropped them off, I was feeling really hopeful and positive—like maybe this was the beginning of a miracle for her. I mean, you just never know. God does work in mysterious ways!

DEAR GOD, PLEASE KEEP YOUR HAND ON JEWEL. I KNOW SHE LOVES YOU. PLEASE HEAL HER AND MAKE HER WHOLE AGAIN SO SHE CAN RUN AND DANCE AND DO ALL THE THINGS THAT MAKE HER HAPPY AND SO THAT SHE MIGHT JUST HAVE A REALLY GREAT LIFE. THANK YOU! AMEN.

Wednesday, June 5 (baccalaureate)

It was so cool to gather with my fellow classmates tonight for a time when God was really honored. Of course, not everyone came (it's an optional service). But (saved or not) the majority of the kids were there (even Trent who not long ago called himself an atheist, although I'm not totally sure what he calls himself now).

Anyway, several pastors spoke, including Tony (who in my opinion outshone them all, but hey, I might be prejudiced). And some really great things were said about letting God lead us from here. So all in all, it was a really sweet time and despite the sweltering heat in the non-air-conditioned gymnasium, it seemed to just put everything into perspective for graduation. I'm really glad they give us this night to look at things from a spiritual perspective because everything can get so wild and happy and crazy on graduation night.

Afterward, my family took me out for ice cream and it was kind of weird sitting there with them (the same ice cream place we've gone since I was just little) and thinking that life as I've known it is about to change for good. I mean, I know I still have the whole summer with them, but once fall comes I'll be living on campus and well, the whole thing just sort of hit me like a ton of bricks tonight. And right there at Baskin-Robbins I started getting all sort of weepy. And before long I had Mom going, and then Dad was wiping his nose. And finally Benjamin pipes up and says, "Sheesh, Caitlin, did you really have to go and make everyone start bawling?" But the sweet thing was I could see real tears in his eyes too. Of course, I pretended not to notice and started joking around, trying to lighten things up. But then as we drove home, from the darkness of the backseat, I told my family just how much I really do appreciate them and how thankful I am for the years they've put up with me.

"So does this mean you're leaving anytime soon?" asked Ben. "'Cause I sure wouldn't mind having your old room, you know. It's bigger than mine."

Then I pretended to sock him in the arm. "No way! Even when I go to college I expect to come home and stay in my old room."

Mom laughed. "We'll see about that. I've been wanting a home office."

And so there you have it. I'm not even out the door yet and people are already making bids for my room. But all joking aside, I know they really do love me. And that's a lot. Sometimes I wonder how people get by without a family to love and stand by them. But then, God's love is big—and I'm sure He can more than make up for anything that's missing. Still, I'm thankful for my family. Probably more now than ever before.

DEAR GOD, THANKS SO MUCH FOR MY FAMILY. I KNOW WE'VE HAD OUR UPS AND DOWNS OVER THE YEARS, AND I'M SURE I'VE BEEN A REAL PAIN AT TIMES. BUT SUDDENLY I CAN SEE JUST HOW SPE-CIAL THEY REALLY ARE, AND I THINK YOU WERE

EXTREMELY KIND AND GENEROUS TO GIVE THEM
TO ME. DURING THE FEW MONTHS AHEAD, PLEASE
HELP ME TO SHOW THEM HOW MUCH I REALLY DO
APPRECIATE THEM. AMEN.

Thursday, June 6 (she's gone)

After struggling for several days with what turned out to
be a severe infection, bad swelling, and finally a cere-
bral hemorrhage, Jewel died today. I still feel shocked
and disappointed to think she's really gone. I mean, I know
she's with God, but it seems so strange that she's not
here anymore. But death is like that. Still, when I think
of her, I can see her smiling childlike face singing "Jesus
Loves Me." It's just so weird.

It's strange to think we were just with her on Monday,
only three days ago. And the following day, she went into
the coma and never regained consciousness. I was
relieved to learn that Tony had gone in last night, after
baccalaureate, to pray with Jewel and her mom. It's like
God had told him, and he listened. Then Jewel died
early this morning.

Part of me says I should be happy for her. I mean, I
know she's with Jesus—seeing Him up close and in person
right now. But still, I feel let down. Here I was praying
(hard!) for her to be healed and instead she died. And I
feel childish and selfish for feeling so totally disappointed. It's like I'm standing down here stamping my foot
and shaking my fist at God. How dumb is that? I mean, I
know He knows what's best. And this isn't the first time my

prayers haven't been answered. But it still gets me. I think I need to go take a walk and just think about all these things.

As I walked around the neighborhood (thinking about Jewel), I remembered what I'd been praying for—a miracle! I'd been asking God to totally heal her and make her completely whole and well, so that she could run and dance and laugh—and well, whatever. And it occurred to me that that's probably exactly what she's doing right now. So it seems God did answer my prayer (just not in the specific way that I'd imagined). And so why should I be all bummed about it? Why should I think I know better than God? And did I forget that He's made each one of us human and mortal—that eventually not a single one of us will escape death?

And so once again I'm reminded that there's just this thin line between life and death—and then after that comes LIFE that lasts forever! And isn't that what believing in God is all about—that promise of something far greater and better afterward? And I suppose when I consider all the poverty and pain and suffering all over the world, I should be incredibly thankful and grateful that there is such a place as heaven. I mean, sheesh, it seems only right!

But I have to admit, as an earthling, I get way too focused on the here and now, and as a result I sometimes forget. I lose perspective. In fact, it's usually only when something tragic happens that I'm reminded of what's important and what's to come. And while it's usually sobering (at first), I am always thankful later on. And so now I'm thanking God that Jewel is with Him. I can see what a complete release that must be for her. Her spirit was light-years ahead of her mind and body, and now perhaps they're all connecting. And so despite my human longing that everything remain the same, I am willing to let go and trust God for eternity—both Jewel's and mine.

DEAR GOD, I ALMOST FEEL AS IF YOU GAVE ME A GLIMPSE OF HEAVEN JUST NOW, REMINDING ME WHAT IS TO COME.... AND IT MAKES YOU SEEM CLOSER SOMEHOW. PLEASE FORGIVE ME FOR GETTING MAD WHEN I FIRST HEARD ABOUT HER DEATH. I KNOW MY ANGER WAS IGNORANT AND SELFISH. I WASN'T TRUSTING YOU. AND NOW THAT I SORT OF SEE WHAT YOU'RE UP TO, I'M STARTING TO UNDERSTAND.

SO DO YOU THINK YOU COULD GIVE JEWEL A BIG HUG FOR ME? TELL HER I MISS HER, BUT THAT I'M REALLY HAPPY FOR HER, AND SOMEDAY I'LL BE UP THERE WITH HER. HEY, I WONDER IF SHE'S MET CLAY YET? MOST OF ALL I THANK YOU FOR TAKING THE TIME TO MAKE SURE THAT JEWEL GAVE HER HEART TO YOU BEFORE YOU TOOK HER HOME. YOU REALLY ARE WISE, GOD. AMEN.

TWENTY-ONE

Saturday, June 8 (recapping graduation)

To say that Jewel's death didn't put a
damper on graduation would be untrue. But someone (I'm
guessing Mr. Myers, our principal) wisely decided to dedicate the first few minutes to her memory. And Joel (who
is valedictorian) was invited to speak some words on her
behalf. And what he said was so perfect and true that I
thought it should be no surprise to anyone that he was
our valedictorian. I know I was extremely proud of him.

   After that, things quickly shifted gears and
announcements of awards and scholarships began. A lot
of the scholarships were complete surprises and there
were a lot of happy kids. And while I was proud to see
both Beanie and Anna go down to receive their college
scholarship awards, I still had to fight down a feeling of
jealousy that I wouldn't be joining them. But then to my
complete surprise the winner of the state essay contest
was announced—and it was me! I mean, I'd totally forgot-

ten all about it (sure that they must've already awarded the prize). And to my complete amazement I was presented with a college scholarship of a thousand dollars a year! Well, I'm pretty sure I could hear my dad let out a whoop of delight from the grandstand.

I walked down to the podium just totally stunned. I mean, to think my quickly written paper about the Mexican kids had actually won! I almost thought I was going to faint (of course, it was pretty hot and stuffy in there by then). But feeling like I'd just won an Oscar or something, I thanked Mr. Myers then found my way back to my seat, and when I finally sat down, my knees felt just like Jell-O. Oh sure, the scholarship isn't big enough to cover the cost of private tuition, but just knowing my writing was good enough to win was a huge encouragement to me.

Joel's valedictory speech was really good, but I think I liked what he said about Jewel even better. Then we started marching down to get our diplomas, and before you knew it, that whole thing was over and we were throwing our caps in the air.

A big group of us went to the all-night party together (even Anna and Joel came along, thankfully not acting too much like a couple). And we just had the coolest time doing geekish things like bowling and playing pool and Putt-Putt, and of course there was lots of eating.

Sometime during the night, Joel got the idea to have a sunrise service (in memory of Jewel). And so a bunch of us (including Natala and Shonda and even Jamal) gathered down at the park. We got into this really big circle and

everyone joined hands; then Joel led us in a prayer and we
sang a couple songs. Then people shared things they
remembered about Jewel. And Beanie told about how we
had sung with her on that last day. And so we decided to
end by singing "Jesus Loves Me." Just as we finished the
song, the sun began to come up. It was amazing. We couldn't
have done it like that if we'd tried. I think almost everyone was crying by then, not sobbing, but just teary eyed.
Then we shared a lot of hugs and went back to the
school in time to have breakfast. And of all the things
that happened during graduation, I think that moment in
the park will stand out to me forever. It's like God was
right there. And maybe Jewel too.

Wednesday, June 19 (the three amigas)

Life has been a whirlwind of busyness the last two weeks.
First of all (after a couple days off), I started my new
job. And I totally love it. I mean, it's kind of exhausting
and some of the kids (especially Terrance the tyrant!)
can really try my patience at times (like nap time when
he refuses to stay on his cot). But mostly it's great. Little
kids are so totally cool. It's like they're so honest—they're
just who they are—they don't play games. (Well, other
than kiddy games, I mean). But even when they're
naughty, it's not like they have any hidden agenda. It's
impossible not to love them. And I can't believe how much
I'm learning. I'm thinking I'll have so much more to offer
the Mexican kids (when I go down in August).

And speaking of Mexico, Beanie has decided to come—and she says she's willing to stay for two weeks! Yippee! But then Jenny found out about it and felt all hurt and left out.

"I can't believe you invited Beanie but didn't invite me," she said one night when the three of us were hanging out at the mall.

I felt horrible. "But Jenny, I only had enough money for one other person, or I would've—"

"So it's about money?" Her eyes lit up.

"Do you think you could come?" I asked. "I mean, would you really want to come?"

"Would you want me?"

"Of course, but it's kind of rough down there." Then I explained in detail about how I'd reacted at first, how I'd been so totally freaked over the deprivation and filth.

"I think I can handle it."

"Will your mom really let you go?" While I knew Mrs. Lambert had lightened up a lot, I still wasn't quite sure how far she could be pushed.

"Mom won't mind. She pretty much treats me like an adult now anyway."

"Do you really want to come?"

"You bet!"

And so it was decided there on the Nordstrom escalator that the three of us would go down to Mexico together.

"We'll be like the three amigos!" said Jenny with a grin.

"Make that amigas," I corrected her. ("Amiga" is the feminine version for "friend.")

"To the Three Amigas!" said Beanie, giving us both a high five.

And now that there are three of us going, I'm thinking maybe I could drive my car (we were going to fly), and then we can give the money we save to the mission. I know it's a long trip, but I think it could be fun. Now, if I can just convince my parents...

Sunday, June 30

I don't know why it's so much harder to keep a diary in the summertime. I guess it's because the sun is calling and there are bikes to ride and pools to swim in (plus ordinary demands like work and mowing the lawn). But it just hit me today that I've been keeping my latest diary for six months now, and I can't believe all that's happened in what is really a relatively short amount of time. (I mean, when you're looking at the big picture.)

Of course, on the other hand, six months in the life of a seventeen- almost eighteen-year-old is kind of like a lifetime of its own. But as I look back, I can see that I've learned a lot. And it's funny because a lot of the time it felt like I was going backward. Sometimes it even seemed like I'd had it more together in the previous year. I mean, I think I've suffered some real identity crises in the past several months. There were times when I felt like I really didn't know who I was or where I was going or anything.

And then last week, when I picked up Chloe (to go to this new Christian coffeehouse in the city where there's a musician playing that I thought she might like—and she did), something she asked me just seemed to help click on the light.

"Do you ever just wonder who you really are?" she asked as we drove.

I nodded. "Yeah, to tell you the truth I've wondered that a lot in the past year. It's like no matter how hard I tried, I just couldn't figure out what I was supposed to do. Go to college or go work in Mexico? So then I finally decide on college but I don't get financial aid for the one I want—the one my friends get to go to. And even when I decide to go to State, I still can't decide on a major. And even then my parents keep pushing me toward writing or journalism, and I still don't know for sure. And, of course, I still think I should do something that would be more helpful in missions. But to be honest, I don't really know what that might be." I sighed in exasperation. "So, yes, Chloe, to answer your question, I am still trying to figure out who I am."

Chloe laughed. "Sorry to get you going."

"No, that's okay." I got thoughtful for a moment, sensing there was some hidden opportunity here. "I guess the thing I've really learned is that I may never completely figure out who I am. And maybe that's not so important."

"Really?"

"Yep. Maybe what really matters is whose I am."

"Huh?"

"Yeah. Because I'm thinking that life will probably always be a little confusing and unpredictable. And I suspect we'll be constantly changing and growing and stuff. But God is constant. And if somehow I can always remember that I belong to Him, then I'm pretty sure everything else will just fall right into place."

Chloe got quiet now and I was worried that I might've gotten up on my soapbox again.

"Did that make any sense to you?" I asked.

She nodded. "Yeah, it actually did."

And so I'm thinking that's it! It doesn't really matter so much who I am (like whether I become a writer or a missionary or a teacher or whatever...), but it really matters whose I am. I belong to God. And knowing that fills me with such a sense of peace. It's like He's the rudder on my boat, and when the waves start tossing me around, I know I can make it safely to the other side.

Because I'm His.

DEAR GOD, THANKS FOR MAKING ME YOURS. PLEASE HELP ME TO NEVER FORGET THAT I BELONG TO YOU—BODY, MIND, AND SOUL. TOTALLY YOURS! WHAT A GREAT PLACE TO BE. I KNOW MY FUTURE'S IN YOUR HANDS, AND I TRUST YOU TO LEAD ME WHEREVER I NEED TO GO. THANKS FOR LOVING ME, GOD. I LOVE YOU!!! AMEN.

The publisher and author would love to hear your comments about this book. *Please contact us at:* www.multnomah.net/diary

a personal note from Caitlin...

Dear Friend,

Do you feel like God is nudging at your heart to make a commitment to Him—any sort of commitment? It's best not to put it off, you know. Hey, remember what happened to me???

So...I invite you to sit down right now before God and consider how He may be leading you. Is He asking you to give Him your heart today? Is He asking you to dedicate your body to Him first and abstain from sex until after marriage? Can you hear His voice speaking to you?

Sometimes it helps to write this kind of promise down. You can do that in your diary like I did, or you can write it down here. Then hide it away if you like, but just don't forget it. Because a promise like this is important—both to you and to God. Because you're His child, and He's always listening.

Blessings!

Caitlin O' Conner

❧ My Promise to God ❧

I, _____, make a vow to God

Print Name Here

on this day _____ that my heart belongs to Him.

Print Date Here

And I make a vow to God, with His help, to abstain from sex

until I marry.

_____

Your Signature

THE DIARY OF A TEENAGE GIRL SERIES
UNLOCKS THE SECRETS OF GROWING UP!

Diary of a Teenage Girl, Caitlin book one   ISBN 1-57673-735-7

It's My Life, Caitlin book two   ISBN 1-59052-053-X

Who I Am, Caitlin book three   ISBN 1-59052-890-6

On My Own, Caitlin book four   ISBN 1-59052-017-3

My Name is Chloe, Chloe book one   ISBN 1-59052-018-1

Sold Out, Chloe book two   ISBN 1-59052-141-2

Road Trip, Chloe book three   ISBN 1-59052-142-0

Face the Music, Chloe book four   ISBN 1-59052-241-9